ACTS OF VIOLENCE

RYAN DAVID JAHN

PAN·BOOKS

First published 2009 by Macmillan New Writing

This edition published 2010 by Pan Books
an imprint of Pan Macmillan, a division of Macmillan Publishers Limited
Pan Macmillan, 20 New Wharf Road, London N1 9RR
Basingstoke and Oxford
Associated companies throughout the world
www.panmacmillan.com

ISBN 978-0-330-51733-1

1 3 5 7 9 8 6 4 2

A CIP catalogue record for this book is available from
the British Library.

Typeset by Intype Libra Ltd, London
Printed and bound in the UK by CPI Mackays, Chatham ME5 8TD

Visit **www.panmacmillan.com** to read more about all our books
and to buy them. You will also find features, author interviews and
news of any author events, and you can sign up for e-newsletters
so that you're always first to hear about our new releases.

For Mary –

with all of my love

Acknowledgements

Several people helped this novel become a reality. Big or small, their contributions to its development are appreciated. Thanks to Will Atkins, Dan Bennett, Martin Bryant, Kevin Finn, Crystal Jahn, Heather Jahn, Dave Morton, Nick Morton, Jacque Morton, Rick Morton, Tony Robenalt and Dave Warden.

And a very special thanks to Mary – you've kept me as sane as anyone could hope to.

RDJ
March 2009

1

It begins in a parking lot.

The lot sits behind a sports bar, a brick building which has been wounded and scarred many times during its long history. It's been hit by drunk drivers who went backwards instead of forwards, had initials carved into it, and been attacked by drunken vandals. Once, fifteen years ago, someone tried to set it on fire. Unfortunately for the potential arsonist, the forecast included rain. And so the sports bar still stands.

It is nearly four o'clock in the morning, three fifty-eight, a dead-dark time before even a hint of light has touched the eastern horizon. Just darkness.

The bar is closed and silent.

Only three cars sit in its usually bustling parking lot: a 1957 Studebaker, a 1953 Oldsmobile, and a 1962 Ford Galaxie with a dented fender. Two of those cars belong to patrons. One of them a door-to-door salesman who spends his days trying to unload vacuum cleaners; the other un-employed, spending his days staring at the cracked ceiling of the apartment for which he's three months behind on rent. Both had a few too many earlier in the night and found other means of getting home, taxi rides most likely. Particularly the unemployed guy. The salesman might have hitched a ride with a buddy, but the unemployed guy almost certainly took a cab. If you have thirty dollars and rent is eighty, there's no point in saving any of it. Drink till you're drunk and pay for a ride home. You might as well enjoy your trip to the bottom. It's when you've got eighty-seven dollars and the rent's eighty that you need to save.

Paper cups and other trash – newspapers, food wrappers – litter the sun-faded asphalt. A whistling breeze pushes the litter across the cracked surface, just for a moment, rearranging the refuse slightly before going still again.

And then a pretty girl – a woman, really, though she doesn't *feel* like a grown-up – pushes her way out the front door of the sports bar.

Her name is Katrina – Katrina Marino – but almost everyone calls her Kat. The only people who still call her Katrina are her folks, to whom she talks every Saturday on the telephone. They live four hundred miles away, but still manage to saddle up and ride her nerves just fine. When are you going to finally wise up and leave that cesspool of a city, Katrina? It's dangerous. When are you going to settle down with a nice young man, Katrina? A girl your age shouldn't be single. You're closer to thirty than you are to twenty, you know. Soon, you won't have the youthful beauty to catch a nice man, a doctor or a lawyer, and you'll have to settle. You don't want to have to settle, do you, Katrina?

Once outside, Kat reaches back through the door, feeling the wall just inside, trying to find a protrusion. Then she does find it, a switch, and she pushes the switch down. Click. The windows looking into the sports bar go dark, and the light which had splashed out into the parking lot, painting the gray asphalt white, vanishes.

Kat pushes the front door closed and locks it, checking the knob to be sure, then swings a metal gate home, bang, and clips a padlock into place.

The gate and the padlock are less than six months old and don't really match the decrepitude of the rest of the place. Also new are bars on the windows. Someone broke in through the back door, emptied the register, took a case of whiskey, and broke out through a window. Why they didn't just walk out the door, no one knows.

The money lost in whiskey and cash was, in the scheme of things, not so big a deal. But the cost of repairs, that was a killer. Plus the lost revenue. The place had to stay closed for two days.

Kat's only the night manager, but she still feels responsible for the place.

As she starts toward her Studebaker, tired, the long night finally catching up with her, the adrenaline of the evening spent, Kat sees that her car seems to be tilting rightward, but at first she can't tell why, or even whether it's real. Maybe it's an illusion, a trick of shadows.

She has to halve the distance between herself and her car before she sees that the tilt is real, that her gee-dee car has a flat tire.

'Son of a gun,' she says, angrily stomping the asphalt, feeling the impact ride up her shinbone.

She makes her way to the car, heads straight to the trunk, slips the key into the scratched keyhole, turns it left, wrong way, then right, hears the lock tumble, and pushes the lid up.

She can't see anything in there.

She fumbles for the flashlight she keeps stored on the left side of the trunk, tucked into the corner there. Her hand bounces around in the darkness for a while before her fingers finally find its cold smooth surface. She wraps her hand around it, flips it on. The light is weak and yellow, but at least it's there. And now that she can see them, she grabs the spare tire and the jack, and as she does, a brief smile touches the corner of her mouth.

Kat's always been a self-conscious person, always sort of watched herself from a distance, and the sight of her, five foot one, a hundred pounds even, wearing a blue wool dress with a white short-coat over it, carrying a tire almost as big as she is, and a heavy jack – the sight of it must have the same effect as a hippopotamus in a tutu. And thinking of that, a smile touches her lips. But it's erased quickly as she thinks of the task at hand.

A moment later, Kat is sitting on her haunches, jacking her car up so she can change the gee-dee tire, watching the wheel well seem to expand while the tire stays firmly planted on the ground – and then finally it starts to lift, the bottom of the tire staying flat. It seems like it should fill with air, expand, as the weight is removed, but it doesn't.

And then – a sound behind her.

She stops moving, hoping that it was nothing, that the sound won't repeat, but it does, and she turns her head to look over her shoulder, afraid of what she might see, but having to look anyway. Kat is a person who's always covered her eyes when the most horrible things happen on-screen at the drive-in movie theater – but she's always sneaked a look through her fingers, too.

Newspaper pages skitter across the asphalt, carrying away yesterday's news.

'Just the wind, dummy,' she says. Just the wind.

She turns back to the car and continues her work.

Kat dumps the flat tire and the diamond-shaped jack into her trunk, not caring how they fall, and slams the trunk lid shut.

It was a nail that caused the flat. The rusted, bent thing was hooking out of the inside wall of the tire like the lone tooth in a mouthful of gums. She vaguely remembers driving through a construction area on her way to work, men with tanned arms carrying broken chunks of wood with shiny nails sticking out of them to the back of a truck, working on repairing a half-burned row house.

Her hands are black with grime, with brake dust, and she's afraid to touch herself, afraid she'll smear black across her light blue dress or her white short-coat. Smear more black. She already managed to get a little on her dress when she carried the tire to the trunk.

Stupid effing flat tire.

She wants nothing more than to go home, slip out of her clothes and into a warm bath, wash herself clean, and then slip again, this time into her bed, beneath her night-cool sheets, where she can sleep till noon, maybe one, and if she's lucky, from the time her head hits the pillow till the midday sunlight coming in through the window wakes her, she'll have pleasant dreams.

But first she's got to get home.

She opens her car door and falls into the driver's seat, sticks the key into the ignition and turns it clockwise. The car groans, the sound of a three-pack-a-dayer clearing his throat. The engine turns over once – slowly.

'Come on, baby,' Kat says.

She pumps the gas pedal.

The engine turns over again, this time a little faster. And again. Gaining speed. She lets off the gas, doesn't want to flood the engine. It turns again. Coughs. Farts. And finally it starts in earnest.

Thank goodness. Kat wipes her brow, glad she won't have to call a cab, and as soon as she does, she remembers the grime on her hands, looks at herself in the rearview mirror, and laughs.

A black smudge drawn across her forehead like on a tramp in a silent movie.

And she can't even wipe it off; trying would just make it worse. But Kat doesn't care. It's been a long night. She worked ten hours straight and she's tired, but all she has left to do is get home.

That's her one last task before the sun comes up.

2

Kat pulls a knob on her dashboard and the headlights create two yellow beams in the night. She can see dust motes and insects floating around in the light and she remembers a time when she was three, maybe four, lying on her parents' bed, which seemed enormous, as big as an island. She was supposed to be sleeping – it was nap time; that's why she was there – but she was awake, looking at a beam of white sunlight coming in through the window, falling on her bare legs. The heat felt good, and she could see dust motes floating in the light. She thought the dust motes were living things. She laughed watching them dance and reached out trying to grab them, but for some reason she never could. They always knew she was coming and floated out of the way of her pudgy fist just before it reached them.

Kat turns a different knob and the radio comes to life. A static-throated male voice, artificially deep, saying, '. . . and

President Johnson said in a statement today that Cuba's decision to shut off normal water supply to Guantánamo Bay Naval Base was unacceptable. In other news, Jimmy Hoffa, who last week was convicted of tampering with a federal jury in . . .'

Kat grimaces, turning the dial.

News is nothing but blah-blah-blah, confirming over and over again that she is small and the world is big, that she can do nothing to stop or even alter the most important things. Kat prefers to focus on things she can change, the lives of the people around her, her own life. Little changes, attainable goals.

Like pouring a drink. Like changing a tire.

'. . . expect a low of forty-two degrees tonight, with early morning showers, and . . .'

Again, she turns the dial.

'Here's Buddy Holly and the Crickets with "Not Fade Away" recorded just two years before Mr. Holly's untimely death. It's hard to believe it's been five years, isn't it? Well, this is Dino on your radio, reminding you that here on WMCA, Buddy still lives.' And then the song kicks into existence with its cardboard-box-banging Bo Diddley beat.

Kat turns up the radio and puts the car into gear.

As Buddy Holly sings from beyond the grave, explaining how it's gonna be, Kat drives through a night city which is filled with silence and hollow, passing a theater advertising

Dr. Strangelove on its marquee; passing a bookstore with a bunch of forty-cent Gold Medal paperbacks piled in its window; passing a stack of dewy morning-edition newspapers tied together with twine and dropped in front of a newsstand which is padlocked shut for the night.

In another forty-five minutes, a fat man with twenty-year-old pimple scars and the matching twenty-year-old anger of someone who got wedgies when he was in grade school will show up, unlock the newsstand, and cut the twine off the stack of newspapers.

The papers claim it's March 13th, but looking at the dark horizon while she drives, Kat knows it won't be March 13th for another three hours or more as far as most people are concerned, no matter what the newspapers say.

She thinks it would be neat if she could stop her car and read one of the newspapers and find out what will happen tomorrow while she's sleeping the day away, but, of course, even papers with today's date only contain old news, news about things that've already happened, things you can never change. Even at four o'clock in the morning.

As Kat drives along a lonely stretch of road, another car, a light blue 1963 Fiat 600, which has been gaining on her for the last half minute or so – she's seen the small round headlights growing with each passing second – zips by with a whistle of wind and the high-pitched squeal of its straining engine and the whine of its exhausted whitewall tires.

A moment after it passes her, Kat turns her car left, onto a night-quiet street, and continues her drive home, south-west toward Queens Boulevard.

Had she continued straight, she might have seen the Fiat moving toward the next intersection. She might have seen the intersection's green light turn yellow. She might have heard the RPMs kick up a notch as the driver of the Fiat strained the small car's small engine further, pressing the gas pedal to the floorboard. She might have seen the yellow light turn red. She might have seen the Fiat fly into the intersection despite the red light. She might have seen a green pickup truck entering the intersection at the same time from the right. She might have seen it slam into the Fiat, right into the passenger's side door, and heard a crash like thunder; seen the Fiat spin; seen it flip as the driver turned the steering wheel the wrong way at the wrong time; seen it roll three times before coming to a stop upside-down on the side of the road, leaving a trail of glass and metal in its wake. She might have seen it sitting there, upside down, in the hollow night air, its sad little tires spinning furiously but gripping nothing, looking like an upended beetle beneath the lunatic moon's yellow light. She might have seen the pickup truck that slammed into it, now with only one headlight, back up, straighten out on the street, and drive away from there. She might have seen the pale face of the driver in the truck turn to the car-nage briefly before driving away. But she never would have known why the driver fled the scene when it was the Fiat that ran the red light. No one will ever know that. No one but the driver of the truck himself.

And, anyway, Kat didn't go straight.

She turned her car left, and continued her drive, which is where she is now – moving along steadily toward home with reflections of herself in the windows of the buildings on both sides of the street to keep her company. Three Kats driving along in the same direction. No way she could see the accident. And when the thunderclap of a crash comes, she doesn't know where it comes from.

She hears it, turns down Buddy Holly briefly and glances in the rearview mirror, and when she sees nothing back there but the darkness, not even a pair of headlights in the distant past looking like wolf eyes, she turns the radio back up, maybe even a little louder than it was before the unnerving sound of the crash, and she continues on.

Maybe what she heard was just thunder. Didn't the man on the radio say there would be early-morning showers?

She looks at the sky, and though it's filled with gray clouds illuminated by the light of the moon, they don't look heavy enough for rain. Not yet. But maybe she's wrong. If so, she hopes she gets home before the downpour starts.

She didn't bring an umbrella.

3

Kat turns her car onto Austin Street.

She can see her apartment complex now.

She can also see one of her neighbors – she forgets his name, a colored man who's always been very nice, who once even jump-started her car for her – pulling his Buick Skylark out of the Long Island Railroad parking lot, turning his car toward her, heading in the opposite direction.

As their cars pass each other, the two neighbors wave.

Frank! She thinks his name is Frank. She remembered as soon as she saw his face clearly, the orange glow of his cigarette cherry floating in front of it like a pet firefly.

She wonders what he's doing out at four o'clock in the morning. She knows Frank's wife is a nurse and often works the night shift – Kat has seen the lights in the apartment lit up when she gets home from her shift at the bar – but she has never seen either of them, Frank or his wife, outside at this time of night.

Kat pulls her car into the Long Island Railroad parking lot, which sits just across the street from her apartment complex, the Hobart Apartments. She pulls the Studebaker into the empty spot Frank's Buick just pulled out of and kills the engine. The sound of the radio dies with it.

Only once has her short drive home from the bar lasted longer than a few minutes – the length of a song – and that was because she took a different route home so she could drop off one of the regulars who spent the last of his cash on a drink and couldn't afford the cab fare. Or to tip her for the drink. Even though nothing bad happened during that drive, it was the one and only time Kat ever gave a customer a ride home. She felt nervous the whole time, her palms sweating as they gripped the steering wheel, but more importantly, she felt it somehow crossed a line that shouldn't be crossed.

A breeze blows through the branches of the oak trees lining the street. A few leaves blow away, but most hold fast.

Kat pushes her way out of the car just in time to see a black-and-white police cruiser roll quietly by, the red light on its roof jutting up like a lipstick. She sees the pale face of the lone policeman inside glancing in her direction, and then he's gone. She watches the red glow of the taillights until the cruiser turns a corner at the end of the block.

In the distance, a car horn honks.

A dog howls at the moon, and then a shout, *shuddup*, a banging sound, the dog yelps, and then silence.

She's tired. Just so gee-dee tired.

Kat believes that people should hibernate, like bears. Winter wears a soul out. If people could hibernate through it, they could wake in the spring refreshed, ready for the rest of the year. They could face it with hope, maybe even optimism. Instead, by the time spring rolls around, as it is rolling around now, people have been made brittle by winter. Cold and brittle. They're ready to shatter.

Kat slams her car door home, sees she forgot to lock it, pulls it open, hammers the lock down, and closes it again.

She can hardly wait for her bath.

But only two small steps nearer her apartment's paint-peeling front door, Kat freezes.

She swallows, afraid.

Suddenly her mouth is very dry.

In the shadows of the night she sees a hulking figure standing near one of the scarred oak trees that guard the front of the Hobart Apartments, that stand between her and her warm bath.

The hulking figure steps away from the tree and moves toward her.

It – he – seems to be pulled toward her, like a magnet, like a yo-yo on a string, seems to glide toward her rather than walk. She doesn't notice the sort of lumbering broken-machine flump-flump-flump a man walking normally has when he shuffles from one place another. He just floats toward her menacingly.

Kat grabs her purse to her chest, as if it were some sort

of talisman, a shield against the night, and she tries to weave around him, to get past him and into her apartment.

And suddenly everything is bright. And loud.

She can see every detail of everything. The pores in the man's skin, large and filled with dirty oil, several blackheads littering his nose. The smudge on his jeans shaped like one of the midwestern states whose names she can never remember and the color of a coffee stain. The flecks of rust on the blade on the knife in his hand standing out like freckles. She can hear the sound of a radio playing somewhere. Muffled talking. A car engine dies three blocks away. She can see a spider on the front door of her garden apartment, building a web in the top left corner. She can hear the bathwater running inside, behind the spider and the front door, filling the tub with warm water into which she'll soon be able to slide.

But that's not real, is it? That last thing isn't real. Not yet. And it won't ever be real if she doesn't get to her apartment.

The man with the knife redirects himself and continues toward her.

But Kat is past him now, in the street, adrenaline coursing through her veins, and she's unzipping her purse, trying to find her keys. A lipstick flies from the purse's open mouth as she fishes inside; it clatters to the street, rolls for a while, and stops. She hears the foot of her attacker crunch atop it with one of his brown leather construction boots. So he must be walking, he must be human, despite the way he seemed to be gliding. Ghosts don't have stained jeans and greasy pores and blackheads, do they? Ghosts don't wear brown construction boots. Ghosts don't need knives. A pink compact leaps out after her lipstick, hits the ground, and Kat thinks she can hear the mirror inside shatter.

Seven years bad luck, she thinks insanely. I'll be thirty-five then.

But now she can feel the keys in her right hand and she's at the front door and she's shuffling through the keys, trying desperately to find the right one, and she's covered in sweat even though the night is cold, and there it is, the right one, the correct key, and she shoves it into the door-knob and turns the knob and pushes the door and the door swings open, come in, Kat, welcome home, and she takes a step toward her living room, toward the safe darkness of her living room, inviting like a womb, like a mother's open arms, and soon she'll be able to close the door on the dangerous world and sink into the warm water of her bathtub and forget any of this ever happened.

Except a cruel fist grabs a handful of her hair and stops her. And that hand drags her away from the front door, leaving it there, open, keys hanging from the doorknob.

I just wanted an effing bath, she thinks.

And then the hand that's not holding her by the hair rises into the night air above her. That hand is holding a knife, a large kitchen knife with flecks of rust littering its blade.

The knife seems frozen in air a moment. Kat can see it in the corner of her eye.

'Please,' she says.

And that's all she says before the knife is hammered down, just behind her collarbone, and there is the grinding sound of metal against bone, and a wet sound, a nauseating liquid moan, and then those sounds are drowned out by the sound of someone screaming – someone screaming loud.

And then the knife is pulled out of the new opening it made in Kat, and she hears a sound like a sword being unsheathed in an Errol Flynn movie. It doesn't seem real. And then warm liquid begins to flow down her back.

She smells copper.

And then another scream fills the air.

I wonder who that is, Kat thinks. Poor thing.

4

Patrick wakes to the sound of an alarm clock ringing and though he doesn't know what he was dreaming of seconds earlier he's sure it wasn't any good because he's got a feeling in his head like wadded-up fishwrap and socks, a sort of dirty ache. His mouth tastes like cigarette ash. His eyes sting.

He fumbles with the alarm clock, not yet awake, just flipping it over in his hands repeatedly and pressing on protrusions as he comes across them. Eventually, he presses the correct button and the clock goes silent. He sets it back down where he found it.

Where am I?

He blinks several times.

Living room. Apartment living room. On the planet Earth.

Who am I?

Patrick Donaldson. Nineteen years old.

What am I?

A human being who's been asked to go to a foreign land to kill gooks – other human beings – for my country.

When am I?

Four o'clock in the morning.

He looks at the TV and sees static.

On the couch beside him, a well-read sheet of paper whose heading makes clear everything that needs to be made clear. 'Order to Report for Armed Forces Physical Examination,' it says.

'Fuck you,' Patrick says back.

He gets to his feet, scratches at himself absently, re-adjusts himself – he got twisted around somehow while he slept – and pulls his underwear out of his ass. He cleans his filthy-tasting mouth with his tongue and swallows.

And then, after one more glance at the Order to Report, Patrick pads across the brown carpet and into the hallway.

'Is it time?'

His mom (her name is Harriette, but, despite the fact that he's technically a grown-up, he still just thinks of her as mom and is pretty sure he always will) looks up at him with her jaundiced eyes, not much more than slits buried in old folds of flesh. She does not look well. Patrick has often wondered how long she has left.

She's only sixty-two. If he dies when he's as old as his

mom is now, that means he's already lived a third of his life. Just about, anyway.

'Is it time?' mom asks again.

Patrick nods. 'It's time.'

'Oh,' she says.

'Yeah,' he says.

Then he walks to a large machine in the corner, a machine that will keep his mother from getting any worse, or at least slow down the process.

That's what Erin says.

Frank and Erin, their next-door neighbors, got it for them. Erin's a nurse. She pulled some strings at the hospital to make sure mom got it because mom said she didn't want to go away and spend the last days of her life in an antiseptic hospital room. She said she'd rather die than live in a hospital room that smelled of solvents, a hospital room from which the humanity had been scrubbed.

Erin also taught Patrick how to operate the thing, which is what he does now.

He pushes the machine over to his mom, then grabs his mom's arm and flips it over, revealing the white fishbelly underside. Revealing radiocephalic fistulae: permanent tubes for the blood to flow in and out of.

Patrick plugs his mother into the machine and gets it started, feeling, as he does every time, like he's in a science fiction movie, like this isn't quite real.

One hour out of every four, he was told.

By five o'clock, an hour from now, mom's eyes won't be quite so yellow; her skin will look almost human.

'You must just be waiting for me to die,' mom says.

'You know I don't mind taking care of you,' he says, which is, most of the time, including now, mostly true. It makes him tired and sad, but mostly he doesn't mind. Besides, he's the man of the house. Who else would do it? His dad bailed on them both when Patrick was ten, went out for the proverbial pack of smokes and never came back.

Sometimes Patrick can convince himself that dad never ran out on them. He was hit by a truck or something, didn't have his identification on him, and from the time he hit the gutter dead his new name was John Doe. From an hour later, anyway, when his corpse was laid out on a cold metal table with built-in gutters around its edges for collecting whatever drains from the dead besides the soul. If dad'd had his wallet, Patrick and mom would have found out what happened to him, but as it was, dad had just been disposed of like every other John Doe since the Civil War: buried in the potter's field on Hart Island. Buried in a trench – in a mass grave, pine coffins stacked three high – without ceremony or individual marker. The end.

Yeah, sometimes Patrick can actually make himself believe that. Somehow that's better than the idea that he just left them. That he just walked away and never looked back. That somewhere his father is alive and laughing with a new wife who isn't ill, with a new son who doesn't look like a woman he ran out on, in a new city that reminds him not at all of the one he left behind.

But then he remembers the day after dad left when he found dad's half-full pack of Pall Malls on the kitchen counter. Went out for cigarettes he already had, huh? Got any bridges you want to sell?

A week later Patrick smoked his first cigarette, sitting alone in an empty alley, hunkered behind some trash cans that smelled of puke and something sweet – fruit, perhaps, beginning to ferment. It made him feel like a grown-up to smoke. This is what men did, and now that dad was gone, he was the man of the house, wasn't he? He would smoke Pall Malls and drink Pabst Blue Ribbon just like his dad.

Only he wouldn't leave mom.

Real men didn't leave.

By the time he got to the end of his first cigarette, he felt sick to his stomach, but he also felt good. His head felt light, like it was filled with helium, like it could float off his neck and up into the air. He imagined his Zeppelin head floating around in the gray city sky. He imagined all the things he could see – the cars lined up like ants waiting to be stepped on, people's rooftop gardens, little corners of the world that couldn't be reached any way but from above. He'd be like a bird up there and there'd be no place he couldn't go.

But real men didn't leave. Not unless they had to.

'Where's your book?' Patrick says.

Mom points.

Johnny Got His Gun by Dalton Trumbo sits on her nightstand next to a glass of stale water.

Patrick picks it up and settles into a chair at his mother's bedside. He moved the chair from the living room two months ago for just this purpose, so he could sit and read to her. It's tattered and old and threadbare and smells like dog even though they haven't had a dog for three years. It's stained and it's got the sag of a man who's lost hope. But it does the job. He flips the book open to its folded page and begins reading.

' "When armies begin to move,"' he reads, ' "and flags wave and slogans pop up watch out little guy because it's somebody else's chestnuts in the fire not yours. It's words you're fighting for and you're not making an honest deal your life for something better. You're being noble and after you're killed the thing you traded your life for won't do you any good and chances are it won't do anybody else any good either."' And then he stops. Licks his lips.

Mom looks over at him with her yellow eyes.

'What is it?' she says.

He doesn't answer.

'Honey?'

Patrick thinks of the Order to Report sitting on the coffee table maybe twenty feet away. He thinks of the edges of the paper already being stained brown on either side from where he's gripped it and sweat into it while reading it so many times. He thinks of standing in his underwear with a long line of other boys who have come to be examined. Raise your arms straight in front of you, palms up; now rotate your arms so your hands face the floor; now touch your toes. He thinks of getting on a bus to some basic training ground. He thinks of bivouacking with the rest of his unit during basic training, learning to survive in the jungle. He thinks of flying off to Vietnam. He thinks of sitting in an airplane seat on his way over, but coming home in a body bag or coffin, stacked up with the others in some cargo hold like so much lumber. He still hasn't told mom.

What'll she do when he does tell her?

Whatever it is, the one thing he's pretty sure she won't do is suddenly get better.

'Honey?' mom says again.

Patrick turns to look at her.

'I don't think I feel like reading,' he says finally.

'You don't have to.'

'Okay.'

He nods, flips the dog-ear back into place, puts the book back on the nightstand, and gets to his feet. He glances down at them, his feet, sees a pink toe, his big toe on his left foot, sticking out through a hole in the sock, and he absurdly thinks, This little piggy went wee-wee-wee-wee all the way home.

'I'll be back when you're done,' he says, and turns toward the door before stopping again and looking at mom.

'If something happened,' he says. 'If something happened and I had to leave, would you be okay?'

Mom shakes her head. No.

For a moment Patrick thinks that's the only response he's going to get, the shake of a head, but then mom says, 'Don't leave me with strangers.'

Patrick smiles.

'I was just talking,' he says.

'Don't leave me with strangers,' she says again.

He nods. 'I'm sorry I scared you. I'll always be here for you, momma. You know that, right?'

Mom smiles. 'I know that.'

'Okay,' he says. 'I'll be back when you're done.'

In the living room, Patrick reads the Order to Report for the sixtieth or seventieth time, then sets it down on the coffee table.

He glances out the living-room window, past the telescope he has sitting there, and out into the lamplit courtyard, which is empty except for four benches and some flower gardens and espaliers and concrete. Then he walks to the telescope and aims it at the apartment windows across the courtyard. As far as Patrick is concerned, the most useful thing you can do with a telescope is spy on your neighbors. They're more interesting than planets; they have more personality, anyway.

At this time of night, though, only two windows are lit up.

He aims the telescope at one and sees nothing but

empty lonesome living room on the other side. A brown and red striped couch. A painting of a galloping horse on the back wall. Probably running away from something. In Patrick's experience, running animals almost always are trying to escape something behind them rather than reach something in front of them.

In the other window Patrick sees a woman sitting alone on her couch. She is forty or so. She wears a black negligee. She is pretty. Patrick thinks that if, when he's forty, he's with a woman who looks like that, he'll be a happy man; he thinks that he'd be happy with a woman who looks like that right now.

But then he sees a trail of black mascara trace down her face and he realizes she must be crying. She blots at her eyes with a tissue. Another trail of mascara does not follow the first.

He imagines himself walking over to her apartment, knocking on the door. She wouldn't open it right away. It's late and there are dangerous people out – rapists and push-in burglars.

'Who is it?' she'd say.

'Your neighbor.'

'Yes?'

'My name is Patrick. I live across the courtyard from you.'

'Yes?'

'Well, I saw you through your window. I wasn't spying.

But I saw you. I saw you crying. I thought maybe you'd like to talk about it?'

And she would open the door. The chain would still be on, of course, but she would open the door so that she could get a look at him, and she would see that he was harmless, that he appeared to be harmless anyway.

She wouldn't say anything. She'd just want to get a look. Then the door would close and after a moment it would open again. This time there would be no chain. She would smile sadly.

'Come on in,' she would say.

'Thank you,' he would say.

After an awkward moment or two she would offer to make hot cocoa, which he would accept, and with their cocoa they would make their way to the couch. They would talk for fifteen or twenty minutes, and she would tell him her problems – but he would not tell her his – and he would put his hand on her shoulder, and then on her thigh, and then he would kiss her and his hand would brush across her breast – accidently, of course; he's not a pig – and it would feel right. She would take his hands in her hands and she would say, 'Let's go to the bedroom.'

'Are you sure?' he'd ask.

She would nod.

5

With the lights on in the living room and the window closed, Diane Myers can see her own reflection staring back at her, as well as through her reflection and into the lamplit courtyard.

It's like looking at her own ghost.

Her hair is carefully done, her breasts held up by the lace of her negligee. Her shoulders are broader than she'd like, but she's grown used to them, and she likes her arms. They're lean but strong, and even though her age now begins with a four, the skin is still milky and smooth. She's wearing a light coat of makeup.

She looks at a clock on the wall, a dumb clock Larry's mom gave them, with a picture of a different animal at every hour, and each time the hour strikes, that hour's animal makes its noise.

It's now eight minutes past four o'clock. Of course. Didn't she just hear the pig oinking, and isn't the pig the four o'clock animal? In another fifty-two minutes she'll hear the cow mooing, and an hour after that, at six o'clock, the cock will crow.

She looks back at her own reflection, at the ghost of herself floating thirty feet off the ground in the courtyard, looking back at her, floating on its own ghost of a couch, surrounded by a ghost of a living room. Is her ghost happier than she is? Being disembodied but still conscious would have its advantages. Walls and locked doors could no longer stop you. No more back pain or neck aches. No more miscarriages with names. Of course, Diane is pretty sure she's finished with wanting to have Larry's baby. Maybe it's even for the best that she never carried one to term.

What happened to their youthful, hopeful love? What happened to the way they always used to hold hands when they walked together? To the way they would look into each other's eyes at random moments and with just that visual contact confirm their love? It seems now that those were two completely different people.

The front door opens behind her.

She gets to her feet and turns around.

In walks Larry. Look at him with his fat fuck belly and his cue-ball head with its mossy half halo of gray hair like cheese that's gone bad. Look at the way he's even gotten too fat for his extra large bowling shirt (it's only a year old), putting so much pressure on the buttons you can see his gut beneath where the fabric from each side of the shirt doesn't quite reach anymore.

Oink, indeed. Hour of the pig, indeed.

Larry nods at her and sets his bowling bag down by the door.

'Hey, honey,' he says. 'Looks like it might rain. You hear the forecast?'

'Where have you been?'

'How about a hello?'

'The bowling alley's been closed for two hours,' she says, ignoring him. 'I've been waiting for you.'

'That's not my fault. I didn't ask you to wait up.'

'Where have you been?'

'Don't treat me like a child who's been out past curfew. Just because we never had kids doesn't mean you need to treat me like one.'

There is silence. Diane is hurt and angry, now, but she thinks that's why Larry said what he said: to distract her with her own hurt and anger, to turn the fight in a different direction. She's not going to allow that to happen. She says again, 'Where have you been?'

He sighs, closes his eyes in exasperation, opens them again, and there's that familiar contempt. It makes her sad.

'Me and the boys went out for a couple drinks after,' Larry says.

A lie.

'You and Thomas and Chris?'

Larry nods. 'That's right.'

'Have fun?'

'It was okay,' he says, and shrugs. It was a way to spend a couple hours, the shrug says, that's all.

'You said you'd be home around two,' she says.

'What does it matter?'

'It matters because I was waiting for you. It matters because I thought we were gonna have a romantic—' She stops, hearing her voice getting shrill. She closes her eyes a moment and collects her thoughts, calms herself.

'Look at me,' she says. 'I look ridiculous.'

'You do not,' Larry says.

What he doesn't say is that she looks beautiful, that he still finds her attractive, that he finds her sexy.

'I do,' Diane says, looking at her ghost of a reflection in the window. 'I'm too old to dress like this and I look ridiculous.' She says it quietly, more to herself than to Larry. But then she turns back to him. 'I want to know where you went after bowling tonight,' she says. 'Can you please just tell me that?'

'Are you implying that I'm lying?'

'No,' she says. 'I'm telling you that I know you're lying – and I want the truth.'

'What are you talking about?'

'Thomas lives on the third floor across the courtyard, third window from the left. His light came on two and a half hours ago.'

'You're spying on my friends now?'

'Don't you try to turn this around. I look for the light

on bowling night because when it comes on, it used to mean you'd be home soon. I wait for you. Tonight I thought it might be fun to . . . I wanted it to be like it used to be.'

'You know why you saw the light at Thomas's turn on over two hours ago? Because his wife doesn't wait up. It was dark in there because *she* went to bed.'

'Thomas doesn't have a wife, Larry,' she says. 'I've never even talked to the guy and I could tell you that.'

Maybe if she'd married a better man she could have kept a child inside her for an entire pregnancy. Maybe her body wouldn't have rejected it as a parasite. Maybe her body has known all along what her mind has denied – until now. Larry is a piece of shit and everything he touches turns to shit. He goes out bowling and drinking and whatever elseing with her money. She works all day at Pete's, waiting tables, delivering burned steaks and undercooked chicken breasts, her ankles swelling, her arms hurting, taking shit from Gary the ass-grabbing manager, while he sits around reading military novels and watching TV, and when she gets home, he leaves, goes out and spends her tip money on beer and who knows what else.

Larry pulls himself out of his bowling shoes and kicks them over toward the door where his bowling ball already sits waiting for next week.

'Of course he has a wife,' Larry says. 'It's practically all he talks about. His wife and his daughter.'

'Don't change the subject,' Diane says, shaking her

head. 'I want to know where you went after you left the bowling alley.'

'You changed the subject,' Larry says.

'Where were you?'

Larry says nothing in response. He pads in his stinky goddamn socks to the window and looks out into the night.

Diane follows his gaze toward Thomas's apartment. She can see Thomas sitting in an easy chair on the right side of his living room. He seems to be staring off into the nothingness. She wonders if he might be looking at his ghost floating on the other side of his living-room window.

She watches him for over a minute. He simply sits and stares. He does not move.

6

Thomas Marlowe sits in his tattered easy chair, still wearing his sweat-stinking bowling shirt and his multi-colored shoes which make him look, he's certain, like a damn fool. Thin gray hair wisps up off his head and thin gray skin-bags sag under his eyes. Gray. He is a man of grays: gray hair, gray eyes, gray moods. The last usually dark gray, bordering on black.

A picture of a brunette woman standing with a young girl of about ten or eleven sits on his coffee table. He looks at it for a long time. The woman has her arm around the shoulder of the girl. They are both smiling. Both of them have blue eyes and straight white teeth. In the background, the Golden Gate Bridge, all the way off in San Francisco. The yellow sunlight is hitting their hair and faces just right. They are beautiful.

There are other pictures of these two throughout the apartment, sometimes together, usually not.

Here is the woman standing in a field of yellow flowers. There is the girl standing in front of the lit-up Eiffel Tower.

Here is the woman holding a fishing rod while sitting on a boulder on the edge of a lake. There is the girl laughing and riding a merry-go-round, hair flowing straight out behind her.

Here is the woman standing on a bridge as a ferry floats by on the water behind her. There is the girl fighting with a dog over a stick.

Thomas is in none of the pictures; he can see himself in the mirror whenever he wants.

His right hand grips the handle of a pistol which is resting on his lap, an ancient Colt .45 that once belonged to his grandfather. It was issued to the man when he was a captain in the army, and it was one of the few things of his that made it home. Also a pair of boots and one round dog tag. Marlowe, William P. 688436. Cptn. U.S.A. The Colt .45 is a semi-automatic pistol but Thomas doubts he'll be pulling the trigger twice tonight.

He lifts it and puts the dangerous end against his temple. The end that promises nothing, which is just what he wants – sweet nothing.

He closes his eyes, trying to find a moment between breaths in which it feels right to pull the trigger, but there's this goddamn music coming from the apartment below, and it throbs through him like a second heartbeat that's not in time with the first.

He stomps on the floor.

'Can't a guy have some fucking peace and quiet!?'

The music gets louder rather than softer.

A woman laughs.

For a brief moment Thomas actually considers storming downstairs, kicking in the goddamn door, and putting a bullet in the brain of any and everyone down there, and then putting several rounds in their fucking record player, watching wood and vinyl splinter and shatter. Then he could have some peace and quiet, then he could find that calm moment between breaths.

But maybe it's not their fault he can't think. He hasn't been able to think all night. Three games and his highest score was one sixty-six. Not good for a man whose average is one ninety.

But then things haven't been good for him for a long time.

He wipes at his eyes and puts the barrel to his temple again.

He thinks of a bayonet in his grandfather's chest, a cardboard box with his grandfather's medals in it, an empty pair of boots.

He closes his eyes.

He pulls the gun away from his head and sets it on the coffee table. He wonders who first called it a coffee table. He gets to his feet and walks into the hallway. He wonders who first called it a hallway. He wonders who first named anything. How did someone look at a dog and decide what to call it? It's all so random. Everything is so goddamn random.

In his bedroom, Thomas finds a stack of bills on the dresser. He doesn't want to write on the bills themselves – he has to pay them – so he grabs an envelope one of the bills came in, blank white on one side, and decides to use that.

Then he laughs.

Pay his bills? How's he gonna do that from the grave?

Still, someone might have to pay them – or at least look at them to determine how much debt he was in when he died. He doesn't really know how that stuff works.

After another minute of shuffling things around on the top of his dresser he finds a pencil and heads back out to the living room.

He looks at the carpet as he walks and he wonders how long it's been since he last vacuumed. There are a few vacuum lines still visible beneath a couple tables, but otherwise all evidence that anyone ever vacuumed in here has been trampled away. Pennies and pieces of torn paper and unidentifiable flakes and crumbs of whatever litter the floor.

He wonders if maybe he should vacuum now, before he gets on with this. He imagines someone will have to clean the apartment, take all his stuff out of here, go through it, see what can be sold to pay off the debts they determined he had by looking at his bills, and so on. Maybe vacuuming would make their job a little easier. Then again, they'll probably have to replace the carpet anyway. Even if he doesn't get any of his brains on it – and he doesn't see how that's avoidable – he'll probably collapse to the floor, and if a week goes by before anyone finds him, he'll have started leaking, and the carpet will be ruined.

Yeah, no point in vacuuming. Might as well just get it done.

He walks to his easy chair and sits back down. He leans forward so that he can use the coffee table as a writing surface, and then he stops. Taps the pencil on the table's surface, thinking about what he should say. He wonders who first called it a pencil.

To whom it may concern, he writes, thinking the formality of the opening is probably the wrong way to go, but he continues anyway with, *if it may, in fact, concern anyone, about which I have my doubts: Nothing tragic happened in my life. You will find no reason for this. You will only find a lack of reason. There was simply no reason to keep waking up. Why get in your car if you've got nowhere to go?*

He signs the note.

He reads it twice, nods to himself, and sets the pencil down.

He picks up the gun and puts it to his temple for the third time.

He wonders why there aren't any good suicide jokes. Suicide is kind of funny when you think about it, kind of ridiculous.

He sits there with the barrel pressed against his head for almost two minutes before taking it away again, setting it down on the coffee table, and getting to his feet.

Thomas has two suits, an okay suit and a good suit. The okay suit is light gray and would be good for a job interview; the good suit is black, made of high-quality fabric, and would be good for funerals and other formal affairs. Thomas wears the okay one. He wants to look decent when they find him, even if he is bloated and the blood has settled to his lower half and begun seeping through the pores like sweat, but he doesn't want to ruin his good suit. They'll need that to bury him in.

He stands in front of his dresser mirror, adjusts his tie, then picks up a comb from the dresser, licks it, and tries to comb down the gray wisps of his hair. They go down momentarily but pop up again.

'Goddamn it,' he says.

He licks his fingertips and tries to force his hair down, but the wisps just pop up yet again.

He can feel his stomach knotting as it does whenever he finds he's lost control of a situation.

Once, about fifteen years ago, he had a string of meat stuck between two teeth, molars way in the back, left side, and he tried and tried to tongue it out and failed, and his stomach started knotting up. So he moved on to a fingernail and tried to dig it out with that, but that failed too. He was having dinner with a woman from work, sitting across from her at a restaurant, so he simply tried to forget it. But he couldn't. And every time his mind drifted to it, every time his tongue accidentally found it, way back there, lodged between the two last molars on the lower-left side of his mouth, his stomach tightened further, he got more sick, he could taste more bile at the back of his throat.

Finally he had to excuse himself. He had to go to the bathroom and really work to get that string of meat out, cursing himself for ordering roast beef, but for some reason it just wouldn't come. He couldn't get his hand into his mouth at the right angle, it was too far back, but he really tried to get his finger back there, to scrape that piece of meat out from between his teeth, and the combination of the nausea from having lost control, from not being able to just get it out, and the reflux from having his hand jammed down his throat, trying to get that string of meat, well, he threw up into the sink.

Fortunately, no one else was in the bathroom at the time and he managed to clean the sink up and rinse his mouth without anyone walking in on him. But he ended up cutting dinner short so that he could drive home and floss that thing out of his mouth, and his stomach was knotted up and sick until he finally did.

'It'll be splattered on a wall in five minutes anyway,' he says to himself now, looking at his hair sticking up in the mirror. And, even though his stomach is tight, he nods to himself.

'You're right, of course.'

But then another thought occurs to him.

He sets down the comb and looks for a pair of scissors.

Thomas is back in his easy chair, wearing his okay suit, his hair trimmed. His eyes are closed. The pistol is in his right hand, pressed against his temple. He lets out a heavy breath and just as he approaches that perfect moment, that stillness between breaths during which the whole world pauses, there is a knock at the door.

He opens his wet, red eyes. He swallows.

He feels disoriented, somehow.

Why is he still alive?

He sets the pistol down on the arm of the easy chair.

He shouldn't have procrastinated so long. Now someone is here. Now he has to get rid of whoever's on the other side of the door before he can go on with it. It's always something, though, isn't it?

'Who's there?'

'How many people did you call?'

'Three or four,' Thomas says, remembering now the series of phone calls he made over an hour ago, 'but you're the only one who picked up.'

'To be fair,' the voice says, 'you called at a ridiculous hour.'

'I knew you'd be awake.'

He walks to the front door, unlocks the dead-bolt, the doorknob, the chain, and then pulls it open.

There stands Christopher, wearing a pair of jeans with folded cuffs, his black bowling shoes, and a bowling shirt that matches Thomas's own. And Larry's. His hair is black with only a dusting of gray at the temples. His eyes are sharp green with flecks of brown. His jaw is square and blue-green with five o'clock shadow. Or whatever time it is.

'What happened?' Christopher steps into the apartment without waiting to be invited and looks around the place. 'Is your wife here?'

Thomas shakes his head.

'No,' he says. 'She's out of town, visiting her sister in California.'

California has always been Thomas's dream place, his agnostic mind's version of Heaven, which is part of the reason he's never gone; he never wanted the dream ruined by the reality and he's always known it would be.

When he was ten, in 1929, when his mom left for good, left him with his grandma (who was lonely since the Great War had made her a widow), she told him she was going out to Hollywood to be a movie star. Over the next couple years, Thomas had dreams of going out to California himself, taking a bus out there. He'd pack a suitcase, take twenty dollars from grandma's emergency tin, and just go. His mom would be easy to find because her name would be in lights and he would move in with her in her mansion that had plush white carpet that felt like seven-o'clock-in-the-morning grass beneath your feet, cool and perfect, and he would never smell the stink of his grandma again, never have to hear her scary laugh followed by her hacking cough as she listened to her radio shows, never have to watch her spit a wad of phlegm into a handkerchief and then fold the handkerchief on top of it as if she were storing it for later.

'Go on and play,' she always said, a lipstick-stained cigarette between two of her clawed, liver-spotted fingers, 'grandma's listening to her shows.'

'What about your daughter?' Christopher says.

'She went to California, too.'

'In the middle of the school year?'

'Spring break,' Thomas says.

'I thought spring break was next month.'

Thomas shrugs. 'Unofficial spring break.'

He pushes the front door closed and slams the dead-bolt home.

Christopher walks to the gun on the arm of the chair and picks it up, flipping it over in his hands.

'What's this?'

'PEZ dispenser.'

'It's loaded.'

'I like PEZ.'

Christopher sets down the pistol and picks up the envelope on which Thomas wrote his suicide note. He reads it.

'Jesus, Thomas,' he says. 'No reason to keep waking up? You have a wife and daughter. I think that's two reasons.

There are people who really do have nothing, but they still keep finding reasons to get out of bed every morning.'

Thomas scratches his cheek and feels beard stubble.

'I should have shaved.'

'What?'

He shakes his head. 'Nothing.' Then: 'I don't think there's anything admirable in staying alive just because. If you've no reason to wake up in the morning . . . I mean, no reason besides work . . . what's the point?'

'You do have a reason. You have two reasons. You have a wife and you have a daughter.'

'But what if I didn't?'

'You do,' Christopher says. 'But if you didn't, then you'd make your own reasons. What you don't do is throw your hands in the air and just give up. You don't just quit.'

'Why not? What's so special about life?'

Christopher looks at him for a long moment in silence, and then says, 'It's all we've got.'

Downstairs, someone changes records and turns the music up further.

Thomas stomps the floor furiously.

'Would you turn that shit down!?' He looks at Christopher. 'I'm ready to fucking kill somebody.'

'You want me to go talk to them?'

Thomas shakes his head, exhaling heavily, calming down – forcing himself to calm down.

'No. They're young and full of life.' He sighs. 'Time'll take care of them.'

'Time'll take care of us all.'

Thomas nods at that.

'So why are you trying to hurry things?'

Thomas opens his mouth to speak but nothing comes out.

7

'You're so bad,' Bettie Paulson tells him, giggling, as he takes his hand away from the record player's volume knob.

And he's never felt so bad in his life – so downright naughty.

If someone had told Peter Adams even a week ago that he would soon be in a room – his own bedroom – with the naked wife of a friend from work while his own wife was in the very next room, well, he never would have believed it.

Peter is thirty-three and clean cut. He has his hair trimmed weekly whether it needs it or not. He has a bit of a beer belly, which is currently flopped out over his white briefs, the only thing he's wearing, but despite the gut and the fact that he's not in his twenties anymore, it's obvious he tries to take care of himself. It's impossible to imagine dirt under his fingernails or a hammer in his hand; he's a man who calls the plumber to plunge the toilet.

Peter laces his fingers behind his head and swings his hips around.

'You love it,' he says.

'I do,' Bettie says.

Peter grabs his whiskey-and-water from the dresser where he set it when he decided to change records. The glass has left behind a condensation ring. Seeing that ring, Peter curses himself for not using a coaster. He considers leaving, going to get furniture polish and a rag. He doesn't want a permanent blemish on the dresser. But then he glances at Bettie, sitting up naked in bed, waiting for him, her teardrop breasts with their large light-pink nipples just asking to be stroked and kissed, and he settles on simply wiping the condensation ring off the dresser with the flat of his palm and then wiping his palm off on his underwear.

He'll take the furniture wax to it tomorrow.

Peter swigs his whiskey and turns to Bettie, trying to forget about the condensation ring.

'Now where were we?' he says.

Bettie smiles naughtily, and a cute little shake shimmies up her spine, and she pushes her chest out just a bit.

'I think,' she says, 'that you were kissing my breasts.'

Peter saunters toward her, smiling.

'Was I?'

Bettie nods.

'Are you sure?'

She nods again.

'Both of them?'

'Mostly the left one, I think,' Bettie says. 'Men always like the left one better for some reason.'

'Well,' Peter says, 'it is a little bigger than the right one.'

'You noticed.'

Peter nods. 'I'm very observant.'

'I guess you are.'

'I can kiss the right one if it's feeling neglected.'

'I think it is,' she says. 'I think you should.'

Peter crawls across the bed, and circles his tongue around the aureola.

'Like this?' he asks.

Bettie leans back and pulls Peter on top of her.

'Like this,' she says.

His drink sloshes in his hand, and he reaches out blindly, trying to set it on the nightstand. He and Anne bought marble slabs for the nightstands a few years ago so they wouldn't need to use coasters on them. It was a smart decision because when one is tired, waking in the middle of the night for a sip of water, one does not always remember to use a coaster. A stone surface eliminates that problem. Peter lets go of the drink, but it misses the nightstand by half, just hits the edge with the clack of glass against stone, and drops to the floor. It hits the floor at an angle, and the impact acts like the hammer of a revolver, shooting the brown liquid and ice out onto the white carpet.

'Damn it,' Peter says.

Another stain to clean up. This one he should take care of now. If he lets it soak into the carpet, it'll never come out. Even if he manages to scrub out the stain tomorrow morning, dirt will always collect there, and every time he walks to bed he'll see that Rorschach smudge and curse himself. He starts to move off the bed.

But Bettie grabs him by the back of his neck and pulls him down to her moist sex.

'Don't worry about the fucking drink,' she says.

Suddenly it's a very easy thing to forget.

'Does your husband do this for you?' Peter asks, burying his face in her folds, in her scent, her black pubic hair tickling the bridge of his nose.

'Not like that,' Bettie says, and pushes her pelvis into his face.

She doesn't look at him when she says it; she is looking out the window and into the courtyard. Her eyes are glassy and far away but she continues to rhythmically grind herself into his face.

He wonders briefly what she's thinking, but then decides he doesn't care.

8

From his living-room window, Frank Riva, a black man closer to fifty than forty, stares out across the courtyard, past his own reflection, past the lamplit courtyard itself, and into a bedroom, where some soft lawyer-type has his face buried in pussy.

Frank wears only a pair of jeans. His torso is bare but for a small patch of black hair on his chest and a barely-visible tattoo above his left pectoral muscle that he unwisely got when he was in the army.

After a moment, he turns away from the window and toward his wife, Erin. She's about five years younger than him and white. She's also six inches shorter than him, her sandy blonde hair cut into a cute bob. She is still wearing her nurse's uniform, which Frank has always found sexy. Even when she hasn't worked he sometimes asks her to put it on before they make love just so he can take it off again. She is also still wearing her work shoes, which is unusual.

She normally has them off before she's closed the door behind her, but tonight she's got more important things than her shoes on mind.

They met in 1943, before either of them had turned thirty, though Frank wasn't far off. He was fresh out of the army and working as a mechanic on Erin's family's farm at the time, fixing tractors and other equipment, living in a shed behind the house and sleeping on an itchy green blanket that he laid over stinking wet hay, using an army duffel bag as a pillow, one of his two pairs of pants its stuffing, brushing away the rats that came out from the hay at night and praying he never got bit, saving up the cash he earned, hoping to start his own business, a mechanic shop, with a sign on the front and everything. That's what he'd been trained as in the army, a mechanic. He spent his two years in the service – January, '41 to January, '43 – fixing jeeps at Camp Gordon, Georgia. He never left the country, never met a German, much less shot one. He first saw Erin three months after his arrival on the farm. She was home from college for the summer. He saw her picking figs from a tree near the back of the house, and that's when she first saw him, too. They both stopped what they were doing and looked at each other. It was a moment and then the moment was over, and Erin's daddy, Mr. Gregory, was asking Frank a question.

'When you think that tractor'll be back up and runnin'?'

'Should have it going within the hour,' Frank said.

But Mr. Gregory must have seen something because he looked from Frank to Erin, and then back to Frank again, and even though Erin had gone back to picking figs and wasn't looking in their direction, Mr. Gregory said, 'You're a good guy, Frank. Hard worker. Honest. I like you, Frank—'

'I like you, too, sir.'

'—but I'll be damned if my daughter ends up with a nigger. No offense to you personally, of course. Like I said, I like you. But don't even think about it. You understand me?'

Frank was holding a wrench in his right hand at the time, and it took all the restraint he had to keep his arm down, to keep from swinging that wrench around toward Mr. Gregory's left temple, to keep from cracking his skull like an egg, to keep looking relaxed and to keep the anger buried deep down where his boss wouldn't see it.

'Frank,' Mr. Gregory said, 'are we clear?'

'Yes, sir,' Frank said.

Mr. Gregory smiled, patted Frank's arm a couple times.

'Good man,' he said. 'I'm glad to hear it. If you was white,' he said, 'I'd introduce you to her myself. I think that highly of you.'

'Thank you, sir,' Frank said through gritted teeth.

Mr. Gregory nodded and walked away, no doubt thinking they'd just had a good talk, man to man, and that they understood each other.

But it was only seven weeks later, six weeks after his first conversation with Erin, that Frank woke up surrounded by flames. Mr. Gregory had found out. Frank didn't know how. He'd only been talking to her. Quietly, sure. About what kind of future they might have together, sure. But only talking. The first time was a week after Mr. Gregory warned him to stay away from his daughter, but after that, they'd found time together almost every day. Someone either told or Frank and Erin just weren't as careful about not being seen together by Mr. and Mrs. Gregory as they thought they were; either way, Mr. Gregory poured gasoline all over his own barn and struck a match. The wood was dry and burned quickly and by the time Frank woke he was surrounded by orange and white flames and the popping sounds of exploding lumber, and parts of the roof were falling down around him, and he was coughing, hacking, couldn't breathe, and his eyes were burning and watering, and he had no idea which way was out, but he stood, stood up blindly on his bare feet, and stumbled, feeling with his arms, going this way, too hot, fire, there's fire there, and then that way, following the sound of squealing rats as they made their escape.

He managed to get out all right. Only his right leg got seriously burned. But he lost all the money he'd spent the last several months saving, lost everything but the clothes on his back. And he had to leave town. If he didn't, he'd find himself strung up from a tree.

But he hung around for two days after the barn burned down, anyway, sleeping in the woods at night. He lurked around during the day, and when he found a chance to get

Erin alone he took it, and he asked her to come with him, to leave town with him so that they could be together.

They headed north that night. Hitchhiking.

They found out quickly that they had to use Erin as bait, and once the car or truck stopped, Frank would come out of hiding. Even then, the driver would often say something about not giving no nigger a ride, nor no nigger lover, and drive off. But the rest of the time they managed to get down the road a stretch. If they both stood out on the road together, though, no one would stop at all.

And now, here they are, twenty-one years later, in trouble again – big trouble.

'Are you sure,' Frank says, 'that it was a person you hit?'

Erin nods at him, panic in her eyes.

'How do you know?'

'I could . . .' She stops, closes her eyes as if to replay the event in her head, and then opens them again and looks at Frank. 'I could see the stroller in my rearview mirror.'

'You hit a baby?'

Erin nods and immediately starts crying.

'Oh, fuck,' Frank says.

Which makes Erin cry harder.

'Calm down,' Frank says. Then: 'Fuck, fuck, *fuck*.'

He walks to the window.

Across the courtyard, he can see a naked man pumping away at a naked woman. The woman is looking out the window, actually seems to be looking at him, her white eyes emotionless.

He turns away. Paces. Turns to Erin.

'Did anyone see you?'

Erin looks up at him, wipes her eyes, smudging her mascara and making herself look a bit like a raccoon. She breathes in and out to calm herself, her chest rising and falling.

Finally, she says, 'I don't know.'

'Of course someone saw her,' Frank says to himself. 'Baby didn't roll itself out into the street, did it?'

He looks up at Erin but she doesn't respond.

'You didn't see anything but the stroller?'

'No,' Erin says. 'I was scared. I just . . . drove away. I'm sorry. I was so scared.'

'So you don't know for sure the baby got killed.'

'No, but . . .'

'Is there any blood or anything on the grille of the car?'

'I don't know. I didn't look. Jesus, Frank, do you think I killed it?'

'I don't know, honey,' Frank says, walking to the window, looking outside, and then turning back to his wife, who he is both furious at and scared for, 'but I'm going to find out.'

He walks to the couch and peels his dirty t-shirt from its arm. The t-shirt is stained with car grease, the armpits yellow with sweat. He flips the shirt right-side-out and slips into it.

'What if someone recognizes the car and thinks you did it?' Erin asks.

'Then I'll let them think it,' Frank says. 'Sometimes people pay for other people's mistakes. You're my wife. I'll pay for yours if I have to.'

Frank grabs the keys from the hook by the door and then pulls the door open.

'I'll be back in a while.'

'When?'

'I don't know,' Frank says. 'If no one is around and the baby is dead, or if no one is around and the stroller is gone, then I'll be back pretty soon. There's nothing I can do in that case, is there? If someone is around and recognizes the car, maybe I won't be back for several years. So I don't know when. What I do know is this. There might be an injured baby on the side of the road right now, and I might be able to save its life. Slim as the chance may be, if I don't go out there and find out, and it is but dies because I'm afraid of getting in trouble, don't you think that puts blood on my hands?'

'I don't know, Frank.'

Frank nods.

'Well, I do,' he says. 'I'll be back in a while. You said it was on the twenties?'

Erin nods.

'Okay,' Frank says.

Then he steps out through the front door and closes it behind him.

9

Behind the wheel of a light blue 1963 Fiat 600 sits Nathan Vacanti, damn near sixty-five, but looking pretty good for his age if he may say so himself, and he may, because he denies himself nothing – almost nothing.

It's just past four o'clock in the morning and Nathan is drunk.

It's amazing how much teachers drink, as a rule. Every time Nathan goes to a party with a lot of teachers, doesn't matter what grade level or subject (though primary school teachers seem to really like white wine, history teachers whiskey, and English teachers merlot or cabernet), he is amazed by the sheer volume of alcohol consumed.

Except for the red taillights of a car about a quarter mile in front of him, he sees no other evidence of active life. The buildings on either side of him are dark. He could be driving through the remains of the apocalypse. Except for the red taillights in front of him.

He grins at the idea of the apocalypse – it'll come if the Russians want it to – and pushes his penny loafer against the gas pedal.

He gains on the taillights.

He turns up the radio, which is playing Buddy Holly and the Crickets. They're doing 'Not Fade Away', recorded just two years before Mr. Holly's untimely death according to the late-night DJ, Dean 'Dino' Anthony.

Now the taillights are only thirty yards ahead of him. Now twenty. Now ten. And now he's passing a Studebaker on the right, and he glances out his side window and looks at a pretty brunette woman, tiny little thing about the size of your average twelve-year-old, and then the only place she exists is in his past because he just left her in his dust.

You'd never know it to look at him right now, drunk as a skunk and needing a shave, eyes veined, lips wet and purple, but Nathan, or Mr. Vacanti as he is used to being called, is a seventh grade English teacher, and has been for the last thirty-two years. He's made some mistakes in that time but he reckons he's done more good than harm. He hopes so, anyway. That's what he tells himself.

Up ahead of him is an intersection, a light-box hanging from a pole, swinging back and forth gently in the night breeze, hanging directly over the asphalt. A bird sits perched on a ledge in front of the green light, a back-lit silhouette. Then there is no green light; there's a yellow light instead. Nathan pushes his penny loafer down to the floorboard, gaining speed.

Yes, he's been a pretty good teacher to most of his students; a few mistakes don't take away from all the good he's done, do they?

The light turns red, but Nathan doesn't even consider stopping. He flies right into the intersection, and he almost makes it across, too, but a large green truck comes at him from the right. Its headlights illuminate the inside of Nathan's car in the moment before collision like the light from a UFO in a B-movie just before abduction.

'Oh, shit.'

Then a sound like the world cracking open fills his head and he's spinning in circles. Everything is a blur of nonsense and lights and pain throbs through his body as it's slammed around the car's interior. He's spinning clockwise and idiotically he thinks if he just turns his steering wheel the other direction he can right himself, but instead the momentum of the spinning and the turn of the tires ends up flipping the car, and suddenly the world is upside down. He can see, momentarily, the single remaining headlight of a green truck shining on him. But then he's right-side up again, looking at the darkened windows of a building, seeing the reflection of his own car in motion. And then asphalt. He can see it so clearly; he can see every pebble imbedded in it; he can see the black smudges of bubble gum pressed into it; he can see where it has been stained by leaking oil. And then it's gone and the world is upside down again. The car rolls three times before finally coming to a stop on the side of the road, down-side up, rocking back and forth ever so slightly. He can hear the whir of his car's tires spinning but gripping nothing. He can hear the tinkling of glass. Through the shattered windshield he can see the green pickup truck that hit him sitting motionless, though rather cockeyed, in the middle of the road, its single good headlight shining on the trail of damage Nathan left behind. Bits of glass, chunks of metal. His spare tire rolls in smaller and smaller circles on the gray asphalt before falling onto its side, wobbling, then going still.

'Help,' Nathan tries to say, but it's only a croak. 'Help,' again, and this time he gets it out.

But the person in the truck doesn't help. The truck backs up, straightens out on the road, and drives away from there, screeching as it goes.

Goes.

Gone.

Nathan looks at the place where the truck should be for a moment, blood running into his eyes from somewhere, and then he tries to open the door, but it won't budge. He doesn't need it to. The windshield is gone; he just needs to get through it.

He spends some time trying to straighten out his contorted body.

There is blood everywhere and he thinks it must be his, there's no one else in here whose blood it could be, but he doesn't feel any pain, and he can't really imagine where it could be coming from. It seems like more blood than a single person could hold.

Finally, he manages to get his body into some sort of human shape, and he crawls out of his car through the shattered windshield, glass digging into the palms of his hands and through his pants into his knees as he goes.

Once out of the car, Nathan struggles to his feet.

Blood immediately pours down his face from a deep wound in his forehead. He reaches up to feel where the blood might be coming from and his fingers brush across what must be a shard of glass sticking out of his head. He considers pulling it out, but decides against it. If he's bleeding this badly with the cork in the wine bottle, it seems the last thing he should do is yank it out.

A bread truck rolls by on its way to making deliveries to grocery stores and Nathan sees the driver's face turn toward him and look, and he tries to raise his arms in a wave for assistance, but before he can the truck has passed and made a left and is gone, heading toward Queens Boulevard and beyond. Nathan can hear the light late-night whine of traffic on that busy road maybe three blocks away, but he can't make it three blocks.

He looks around at the darkened buildings, all businesses so far as he can tell, but business hours have long passed. He could knock on every door on the street and never get an answer. And he doesn't have the strength to knock on every door, anyway.

He stumbles, bleeding, toward a window with bicycles displayed behind it. As he nears the window, he looks for something with which to shatter it. A rock would do, but he doesn't see a rock. Then he reaches the window and presses his palms against it, smearing blood across its cold, smooth surface. He can see his own reflection looking back at him. He can see several inches of bloody glass jutting from his forehead like a shelf. He wonders if it's in his brain, and suddenly his head is throbbing with pain. Has it been throbbing this whole time? He thinks so. He thinks every part of him is probably in pain, but the mind simply can't handle pain everywhere, so it picks focal points, and seeing the shelf of glass jutting from his forehead made his head just such a focal point.

Suddenly Nathan feels very sick. Dizzy. He has to get inside that store before he passes out. He has to get inside, and he has to call for an ambulance. Or he's a dead man.

He looks around again for something to break the window with, and again he finds nothing. He looks out toward the street. Another vehicle passes – this one a Cadillac Fleetwood driven by someone so small Nathan can't figure out how the guy can see over the dashboard – and the driver looks toward Nathan, and Nathan waves, but the car doesn't slow down. Nathan is pretty sure the car actually speeds up. And then it's gone. He'll just have to punch his way through the glass. He's already cut to shit; he can't imagine the damage caused by the store's window making it much worse.

He pulls back and punches, and the window bows in and makes a strange saw-like warbling sound, bouncing back, vibrating, shaking the reflections of Nathan and the street behind him like a horse trying to rid its hide of flies.

Light from the moon bounces off the glass jutting from his forehead; he can see it in the warbling window. How deep is it? Is there another six inches of glass inside his head, deep into his brain? Has he just gotten a car-wreck lobotomy?

Jesus fuck.

He falls to his hands and knees, sending sharp pain into his body as small shards of glass already imbedded there are pressed further into him, and he vomits onto the sidewalk. His entire body tightens with each gush, his mouth locking open, and his body evacuates itself in three contractions.

Then it's over.

He breathes hard, spits, blows his nose onto the sidewalk.

He's going to die out here. That's all there is to it.

But then he sees it. The metal-framed sandwich-board sign sitting out on the sidewalk. Apparently there's a spring bicycle sale on. Apparently every bike in the store is twenty percent off. Every fucking one of them.

Nathan struggles to his feet. Limps to the sign.

Has it been here the entire time? Dumb question. It has to have been.

He picks it up with his bloody hands, spins his entire body around, toward the window, and lets go. As he lets go, he continues a half spin and falls to the sidewalk a second time.

He looks up.

The metal-framed sign fumbles through the air in a weak arc, hits the window, and then simply drops to the sidewalk like Wile E. Coyote after he's noticed he's past the cliff's edge and is walking on air. It clatters a little as it settles, and then goes silent. The window warbles again, but seems to hold together.

'Oh, goddamn it,' Nathan says. 'Fuck.'

He's going to die out here.

But then the window splinters – just a small pinpoint crack where the sign made impact at first, but then it splinters – and the splintering spreads, spiderwebbing in every direction, out and out from the point of impact, and pretty soon the entire window is covered with cracks. Pretty soon you can't even see through it – it's just frosted with cracks – and pieces, small pieces, start to fall out, tinkling to the ground like snowflakes.

Nathan grabs chunks of shattered glass and pulls them away, not caring if they cut his hands more than they're already cut – he wants to live – and then crawls into the darkened store, falling over bicycles, picking himself back up, crawling his way in.

He sees a telephone hanging on the wall behind the front counter, stumbles to it, picks it up, puts it to his bloody ear and dials an operator.

'Hello,' he says. 'Help. I've been killed in a car accident. Please. Please.'

He might even manage to give his location before he's gone. But then there's just blackness for him, and the sound of his own body crumpling to the floor.

Then silence.

10

Frank walks from the Hobart Apartments and toward the Long Island Railroad parking lot across the street. He's thinking about a knocked-over stroller on the side of the road only a few miles from here, thinking about that stroller and what might be strapped inside it, but as he walks he sees a man standing in the shadows, leaning against the trunk of an oak tree, smoking. He sees the orange glow of the cigarette in the night, the whites of the man's eyes.

'Excuse me,' Frank says. 'Sorry to bother you, but do you think I could bum one of them smokes from you?'

The orange glow of the man's cigarette bobs up and down and a moment later a pack of cigarettes juts out of the shadows. Frank takes one.

'Thank you,' he says, loading the cigarette between his lips. 'Think I could get a light?'

A flame flickers into existence. Frank lights his cigarette on it.

He also sees the other man's face for the first time. He's a black man with bloodshot eyes and a nonexistent chin that looks like someone hacked it off at a forty-five degree angle with a machete and a nose shaped like a tipped-over three. It's a face you could forget – except there's something wrong with it. Frank isn't sure what exactly. There's nothing to point to – that there's the problem, sir; I'll have it fixed in a jiffy – but the combined parts are somehow almost disorienting, like an optical illusion, like something Escher would create.

Then it's gone, and the man's hand is pulling the lighter back into the shadows.

'Thank you,' Frank says, wondering what this guy is doing standing in front of his apartment complex at four oh something in the morning. But it's a big complex and for all Frank knows the guy lives here too and just came outside for a breath of fresh air. Besides, he's got more important things to worry about.

He takes a drag from his cigarette and crosses the street, heading toward his 1953 Buick Skylark, its white canvas top up, its red paint beginning to oxidize but still managing a little shine beneath the moon's pale light. The car's a little rusty around the edges but it's in pretty good shape nonetheless. Someone brought it into his shop on Forty-seventh Street five years ago to have the transmission worked on and never returned. Frank claimed it.

He lets himself take one more look over his shoulder at the man with the bad face before he arrives at his car. Then he finds a flashlight in the glove box – which has never seen a glove as far as Frank knows – and walks around to the front of the car.

He flips the flashlight on and drags the beam across the chrome front of his car. There's a fist-sized dent there, on the right side of the bumper. Fist-sized – or maybe about the size of a baby's skull. It's a shallow dent, a couple centimeters deep at most, a dent that might have been there for years. He's just never been a man to look for things like that. He regularly tunes the car up, or has one of the boys do it, but a dent here and there is nothing he's ever paid attention to. And yet, he's almost certain the dent is new – less than an hour old – and about the size of a baby's skull.

He turns the flashlight off and puts it back in the glove box. He walks around to the other side of the car and squeezes his large frame in behind the wheel. He sits there a moment thinking.

About the size of a baby's skull.

Then he sticks his key in the ignition and starts the car. Looking over his shoulder, he backs out of his parking spot, shifts into drive, and turns left onto Austin Street.

Buddy Holly is on the radio, singing 'Not Fade Away' but that's the last thing on his mind.

At least he found no blood or hair or flesh.

As he drives down Austin Street, he passes one of his neighbors in her Studebaker. He thinks her name is Katrina, but she goes by Katy or Kat. Something like that, anyway. He jump-started her car for her once. He waves and smiles behind his cigarette – as if I'm just heading to the store to get a bottle of milk, he thinks – and Kat waves back at him. Then they've passed in the night.

Frank glances in his rearview mirror and sees Kat's Studebaker pulling into the Long Island Railroad parking lot, pulling into the spot he just pulled out of, and then he makes a right onto a side street, passing a cop car which is making a left off of it. Which is making a left onto Austin Street. Which is now driving toward his apartment complex.

What if the fuzz are coming for Erin?

Frank pulls the Skylark to the side of the street, puts it in park, and, leaving the car running and his door open, walks to the corner so he can look down Austin Street, so he can see where the patrol car is heading. It continues on past the Hobart Apartments without even slowing and keeps on moving, taillights shrinking.

Thank God.

Frank allows himself to breathe, heads back to his car and gets inside. A moment later, his left turn signal click-click-clicking, he pulls back out into the street and continues on.

11

Inside his police cruiser, Officer Alan Kees makes a left onto Austin Street and continues on at about fifteen miles per hour. He glances toward a parking lot as he drives and sees a pretty brunette woman just getting out of her Studebaker. He considers having a little fun with her – your left brake light's out, ma'am; normally I'd have to write up a ticket, but I think we might be able to work something else out – but decides against it. He's got business to attend to elsewhere, and besides, she looks like a fighter, which always turns ugly.

He drives by without giving her another thought.

When Alan Kees joined the police force five years ago, at the ripe old age of twenty-two, he actually had an idea that he might be able to do a little good – protect the citizenry, keep them safe – but within six months, the idea seemed nothing but a quaint concept for a more innocent time. He realized quickly that there are two kinds of people in the city: cops and everyone else. And everyone else just can't be trusted. Cops might lie, they might steal, but they've got your back. If you get put into a corner, there will be another cop there with a sledge hammer, banging an escape hole through the lath and plaster – and ten times out of ten it's a civilian that gets you backed into that corner in the first place, not another cop. It ain't just the criminals, either. Those asshole civil libertarians (commies, more like it, if we're gonna call a spade a spade) at the ACLU and other organizations with their screeches and cries about rights and police abuse and other nonsense are just as bad. They're worse. You can at least understand your criminal. Their motives are clear and obvious. They live in a hard world where you grab what you can and you hold on to it as long as you can, and if someone tries to take it away, you view that as a threat to your life and you go at them red in tooth and claw and you don't stop when they're down – no fucking way, pal – you only stop when they're no longer capable of getting back up, you only stop when they're down for good, even if that means putting them under a half ton of moist soil.

Think of God's red right hand.

That's what Detective Sampson told Alan five years ago when he first entered the force, and when he asked Sampson what that was supposed to mean, Sampson said, 'It's from Milton. He calls the vengeful hand of God His red right hand. Well, if God's right hand is red, is violent, is vengeful,' he slurred here, a little drunk, always a little drunk, 'then those who grab the most power through violence are closest to God, aren't they? Remember that. The criminal is closer to God than any of those goddamn pacifists will ever be – than they'll ever understand. Respect the criminal enough to kill him, Alan, because if you don't, he'll kill you. He'll kill you and he'll be the one standing at God's side when it all comes down. Read the Old Testament. God respects nothing so much as violence.' He stared off at the corner for a minute here. 'Read the Old Testament,' he said again, and then took a hard swallow from his flask, his throat making a clicking sound as he did.

Alan nodded, but he didn't really understand.

He understands now, though.

Alan pulls his police cruiser to the curb behind a Ford F-100 ambulance which is already parked in front of Al's Coffee Shop. The driver sits waiting for his coffee and donuts, looking at himself in his sideview mirror, picking at his teeth with a match book. Probably sent his partner in for the goodies. One of the benefits of being the driver on an ambulance team. That and the extra few cents an hour.

Alan pushes his door open and steps from the car.

He walks by the ambulance and its driver, who's still picking away at his goddamn teeth.

'Keep up the good work,' Alan says as he walks by.

The driver gives him an ironic salute.

'You too,' he says smiling. And then, after Alan has taken a few more steps, 'Asshole.'

'I heard that.'

'Good,' the guy says. 'Now you know what I think of you.'

Alan fights a violent urge, and turns away from the ambulance, gritting his teeth.

Last time Alan went to get his teeth cleaned his dentist commented on his grinding problem. 'You're gonna end up with nothing but nubs by the time you're sixty.' As far as Alan is concerned, nubs are enough – as long as they're sharp and can tear out a throat.

He pushes his way into the coffee shop.

Duke stands behind the counter, handing a couple coffees to a uniformed paramedic in his mid- or late-thirties. The guy looks like he hasn't slept in a decade. Bags under his eyes like pig-bladder canteens.

'Nice friend you got out there,' Alan says.

The paramedic looks at him, says nothing.

'Will that be all?' Duke asks.

Although the place is called Al's Coffee Shop, no one named Al has been involved in running it for at least fifteen years. Duke is the owner-operator. Alan once asked Duke how he came up with the name and Duke told him that's what it said on the front when he moved in back in '49 and he saw no need to change it – so Al's it was and Al's it is.

The paramedic continues to scan the case of donuts.

'Um,' he says. 'Let's see.'

'Take your time,' Alan says. 'It's not like anyone's waiting.'

And then there's a yelp of siren and a brief flash of light from the ambulance on the other side of the window.

The guy looks over his shoulder, then looks back to Duke. 'Guess that's it,' he says. 'How much?'

'On the house,' Duke says. 'Go save some lives.'

'Thanks. 'Preciate it.'

Then the guy heads out the front door.

Alan watches him jump into the ambulance through the passenger's side, and then the thing wheels off, all lights and noise.

Once the ambulance is gone Alan turns to Duke. 'How 'bout a large coffee, huh?'

'No thanks,' Duke says. 'I'm wired as it is.'

'Smart ass. Pour me my cup.'

Duke turns around, grabs a paper cup off a large stack of them, and pours.

'Donut?'

Alan shakes his head. 'Any messages for me?'

'Your phone rang,' Duke says, 'but I couldn't get to it.'

'Couldn't?'

Duke nods.

'You couldn't get to it.'

'That's right,' Duke says.

'What's so important you couldn't get to the fucking phone?'

'Had a turtle-head poking out.'

'What?'

'I was taking a shit, Alan.'

'Well, I hope you washed your fucking hands.'

Alan grabs a dime from the tip jar and, with his coffee in hand, heads back out into the night. He heads toward the phone booth he uses to conduct business, but some guy is hugging the corner of the thing, his back to the open accordion door, whispering loudly into the mouthpiece about you bitch, I can't believe you fucked my brother after all I did for you, I'll fuckin' kill you for this.

Alan walks over, stands on tiptoe in order to put his coffee on top of the booth, and then taps the man's shoulder.

The guy turns around and looks at Alan with blazing eyes which are pressed into the doughy, pockmarked face of a man plagued by boils. There's one above his left eyelid that looks ready to burst, in fact – hanging down over the eye like a gourd – and Alan decides that's where he'll punch first if it comes to blows. That would be some serious pain.

'Can't you see I'm on the fucking phone?' Boil says, and then he sees Alan's uniform, and his face blanches. He covers the mouthpiece with his hand. 'Sorry, officer. I didn't realize it was you.'

'Do we know each other?'

'Uh, no. I just mean I didn't know you were a cop. A policeman, I mean.'

'Cop is fine. Didn't I put you in jail before?'

'No, sir.'

'You sure?'

A nod.

'Well, you're on my phone.'

Boil looks confused. 'I'm sorry?'

'You don't have to apologize,' Alan says. 'Just hang up the phone and walk away.'

'I don't think I understand.'

'Hang up the phone,' Alan says, 'and walk away.'

He walks his fingers across the air to demonstrate.

Boil nods and his moonface shakes like gelatin, mouth agape. He hangs up the phone without saying goodbye. Then he looks at Alan as if awaiting further instruction.

'Walk the fuck away.'

Boil nods, 'Right,' then turns and heads off down the sidewalk. He glances once over his shoulder, but only once, and Alan thinks it's fear on his face, nothing more. And fear is fine.

Alan grabs his coffee and then steps into the booth. He picks up the phone, wipes it off on his uniform. He doesn't think boils are contagious, but that was one filthy son of a bitch. Once the phone's wiped off, he drops his dime into the coin slot and dials.

'Charlie. Alan. What's the news?'

He takes a bitter mouthful of coffee and nearly spits it right back out, but manages to swallow. It goes down hard, like a stone.

'He what? That motherfucker. Where'd he say to meet him? Tell him I'll be there.'

Alan slams the phone down and steps from the urine-stinking booth. He looks at the coffee in his hand as if it's an alien thing and then throws it against the brick wall in front of him. It explodes, splashing liquid in every direction, including onto Alan.

'God *damn* it!'

He kicks at the booth several times, grabs it, tries to shake it but it's bolted to the concrete, steps back into the booth, grabs the phone, and repeatedly slams it into its pronged cradle until there's nothing left of it but three mangled pieces of plastic held together by wires.

'God fucking *shit* fuck!'

He runs his fingers through his hair, tilts his head left to crack his neck, and then tilts it right, producing a sound like a playing card flapping against bicycle spokes.

About six months ago Alan and Charlie decided to shake down a local drug dealer for a little extra cash. They thought it was a small-time operation: figured the guy had five or six people working for him who were throwing his mediocre shit to the niggers and spics. They figured on an extra forty dollars a month. Hazard pay, they called it. But when Alan and Charlie put the guy they thought was top in a corner, he squealed like a pig, oh God, man, please don't send me to jail, I got six kids (six fucking kids) I gotta take care of, oh man, this is fucked, I'll tell you whatever you wanna know, I swear, I'll fucking talk.

Now Alan and Charlie didn't even know this dumb son of a bitch had anything worth talking about till he told them he did, but they went along with it, of course. What else are you gonna do? Someone starts telling you an interesting story, you listen to the end. The story led them to a bigger fish, who they paid a visit to the next day. At first Big Fish claimed he didn't know what they were talking about, he's a respectable businessman, the whole line of shit. But Alan can be persuasive when he needs to be, and he really laid on the charm, laid it on with a ballpeen hammer, first breaking the pinky toe on Big Fish's left foot, and then the next toe, and then the next. Before Alan could get to the guy's last toe, Big Fish was talking plenty, would have told them anything, would have told them his very own mother was a ripe cunt.

So they managed to work out a pretty good arrangement, a pretty good deal that everyone seemed happy with: three hundred dollars a month to both Alan and Charlie and Big Fish gets to keep his operation going. Not a bad arrangement – not bad at all.

Except now, after six months of everything running smooth as a baby's ass, there's a problem.

Some son of a bitch calls up Charlie at home two days ago – doesn't explain how he got Charlie's home number either – and claims he knows what's going on, has seen it several times from his office window across the street. Claims he even brought out his Bell and Howell Zoomatic and filmed them making a collection. Claims it's damning evidence, what he has on film. Claims he can get 'em kicked off the force, maybe even put 'em in jail.

'And you know what happens to cops in jail,' he says.

But he says he'll sell it to them, the film he's got. Sure. He knows the salary of a cop isn't great. He understands the need to make a little extra cash. Hell, he says, he's a reasonable man, and he'd like to make a little extra cash himself.

Charlie says all right, they'll make a deal and collect the film and that'll be that. What's his price? The guy hesitates, then says he'll call back once he's had time to think about it, he'll call back tonight – which is what Charlie's been sitting around at home waiting for – and now he has called back, and he's named his price. And that's where the real problem is. Now Alan has to reason with the guy, and based on his price, he's not the reasonable man he claims to be.

Alan runs his fingers through his hair again, glances at his coffee, which is now splashed across the brick front of Al's Coffee Shop, and he heads back inside.

After Duke has poured Alan another cup, he decides he'll have a donut after all.

'Maple-glazed Long John,' he says, and Duke grabs it for him.

'I really hope you washed your fucking hands.'

He's halfway to his car, mouth full of donut, when the sound of a scream pierces the air. He stops a moment, takes another bite, listens, hears another scream. He considers it for only a moment.

'Let someone else deal with it,' he says. 'I got shit to do.'

12

Peter is on top of Bettie, his hands holding her arms down against the mattress, pushing fingertip bruises into her soft flesh. He can feel the jack-in-the-box buildup of orgasm almost ready to explode from within him. His hair is sweaty and hangs down in his face, dripping saltwater onto Bettie's breasts. And then the orgasm arrives and he thrusts hard into Bettie, forcing all of himself into her one, two, three, four times, hearing her groan, holding himself in her with the last thrust, and then he's done, and he's breathing hard, his heart pounding against the wall of his chest like something trying to escape, like a trapped hummingbird.

He wipes his hair away from his face and looks down at Bettie, smiling, but she is not looking back. It's as if he's not here at all. She is looking out the window.

'Did you hear that?'

Peter pulls himself out of her, going flaccid quickly.

'Hear what?' he says.

'That scream.'

'I didn't hear any scream,' Peter says, 'except from you.'

But her mind doesn't seem to be on sex anymore.

'Are you sure?'

'Yeah,' he says, 'I'm sure.'

'I heard a scream,' she says. 'Two screams. I'm sure of it. I'm positive.'

She stands, wraps a sheet around her naked body, and walks to the window to see if she can see the source of the screams she says she heard. Then she glances down at herself and uses the sheet to wipe the inside of her thighs which are, apparently, dripping.

Peter wants to ask her not to do that – to please use a wash cloth; those are high quality silk sheets and she may be ruining them – but he bites his tongue.

Now isn't the time.

Patrick is simply sitting on the couch and looking at the static dance across the television's gray surface when he hears the screams. One second he's trying to imagine himself in a camouflage battle-dress uniform and jungle-boots, a rifle in his arms as he wades through a rice paddy looking for gooks, the next second he's snapped out of his thoughts and back into reality by what sounds like a dying animal.

He stands and walks to the living-room window.

He sees several apartment lights turning on, he sees several human shapes moving to their windows, some of the shapes alone, some of them standing in twos. In one window he sees a woman, a man, and a small child, maybe six years old, all standing together like in a family portrait.

Larry's telling Diane that he's tired and he just wants to go to bed, can't they talk about it in the morning – the evasive son of a bitch – when the screams come, and Diane momentarily forgets the fight and turns toward the window, and then walks to it for a better view.

The lights in the courtyard make it possible to see out fairly well even though it's night, but Diane doesn't see anything, just empty space. Four benches, some flower beds, and concrete.

A moment later, Larry is standing beside her.

'What is it?' he says.

'I don't know.'

'Sounded like screams.'

'Or a dog yelping.'

'It sounded human.'

'Are you sure?'

'No.'

'I think it sounded like a dog yelping.'

Thomas and Christopher both walk toward the living-room window, closer and closer, until their reflections and the reflection of the living room surrounding them disappear, and they can see the courtyard clearly, without having to look through themselves.

'Maybe we should turn off the light,' Christopher says.

But neither of them move to do so.

'I'm gonna go see if Ron and Anne heard anything,' Bettie says, turning away from the window and looking at Peter, who seems bemused, who is simply sitting on the edge of the bed, staring into the ether.

'Okay,' he says without looking up at her.

'Are you all right?'

He nods.

'You sure?'

He looks up at her and smiles.

'Yeah,' he says. 'I'm sure.'

'All right,' she says, stroking his face. 'I'm gonna go see.'

'Okay. I'll be out in a minute.'

She walks to the door, pulls it open, and then walks through it.

In the living room, Anne, Peter's wife, who Bettie thinks is a sweetheart, and Ron, Bettie's husband, stand in front of the living-room window. Both of them are motionless as statues; they simply stand there, looking out.

Bettie says, 'Did you guys hear that?'

'Sounded like screaming,' Ron says, turning to look at her as she walks up to him and puts an arm around his waist. His body is warm against hers, and a bit sticky, and he smells of sex. The entire living room smells of sex. Bettie glances at Anne, who is wearing a thin pink robe, and then she looks out the window.

'Have you guys seen anything?'

Anne shakes her head.

'Not yet,' she says. 'Oh, wait, there.'

She points.

'I think I see something too,' Bettie says.

Peter walks out of the hallway in a pair of wrinkled slacks, his pale belly shirtless.

'What is it?' he asks.

13

Kat crawls out of the night shadows that have laid themselves across the street-side of the apartment complex and makes her way into the lamplit courtyard. She is pulling herself forward on her arms, which scrape and bleed against the concrete beneath her. But she doesn't care about the pain in her arms; she just wants to get away from the man with the knife.

She just wants to get away.

Her shoulder itches. She thinks he stabbed her. There's a burning sensation inside her, behind her armpit, and she thinks he stabbed her.

She struggles to her feet, first getting them flat on the ground beneath her body and then using her arms to push herself up. She looks over her shoulder into the darkness but does not see the man with the knife nor the glimmer of the blade.

Maybe he left. Maybe the lights in the courtyard scared

him. Maybe he didn't want to be seen and he left. She would be okay then. She would be okay if he just left. Someone could fix her up, make her stop hurting, and she would be okay.

She looks around the courtyard. It's about thirty feet wide and fifty feet deep and concrete except for a round flower garden in the middle and a few half-circle flower gardens along the edges where the concrete meets each of the four buildings that make up the complex. There are four benches surrounding the central flower garden. The buildings themselves stand five stories high. Kat has no idea how many apartments are in the complex but she knows that about half of them look in on the courtyard and she sees that several of the windows are lit up. She has never seen so many of the apartments with their lights on when she's come home from work. There must be a dozen living-room lights on. There must be thirty or more people standing on the other side of lit and unlit windows. She can see their faces looking down at her.

She can see the whites of some of their eyes.

'Help,' she says. 'Someone help me.'

She looks at the faces of the people in their apartments, and they look down at her. She recognizes some of them: Larry and Diane Myers in their second-floor apartment; and Thomas Marlowe, who helped her carry her groceries inside once; and Anne Adams, who, because Kat is Italian, always asks her about pasta sauces. There are dozens of others. She can see them looking down on her through their living-room windows as if she were nothing more than an image on a television screen. And how many can't she see? How many more are standing and staring at her from far back in their darkened living rooms, out of sight?

'Help,' she says again.

She hears the sound of footsteps behind her and she looks back over her shoulder, and the first thing her eye sees is a tear in her white coat – no not a tear, a cut, a slice – and it's leaking a dark burgundy liquid that smells like metal tastes, and then she looks past her own shoulder and she sees him. Oh God. I'm sorry, God, I didn't mean to take your name in vain; I'm just so gee-dee scared, and I hurt so bad, and there he is. Oh God, he didn't go away – he didn't go away. He didn't go away. Oh God, get me out of this. The man with the rust-spotted knife walks out of the shadows. He is six feet tall and he must weigh a hundred and eighty pounds and his eyes shine with malevolence and his right hand is holding that big kitchen knife and his brown construction boots are speckled with blood. With her blood.

He walks toward her.

Kat starts crying.

'Oh, God, no. No,' she says. 'Please – please. Please,' she says.

But he keeps coming for her. The man keeps walking and no one does anything to stop him. They just stare from their living rooms. They just look down at her with their wide white eyes.

Then he's here, the man with the knife, and he grabs a handful of her hair in his fist. She can smell his sweat. She can see the blackheads on his nose. She can see the veins bulging in his neck, and she can see veins in his eyes like fire coursing down the side of an active volcano.

He throws her to the ground.

14

Thomas pulls down the window shade, blocking his view of the terror below. He couldn't see everything that was happening, but he saw enough to know he couldn't stand to see more.

'I can't watch that,' he says.

'I know what you mean.' A pause. 'Should we call the police?'

Thomas thinks about it a moment, and at first it seems like the right thing to do, but then he remembers all those faces he saw – standing, staring down at the courtyard from their living-room and bedroom windows; dozens of faces, dozens of them – and he thinks of the police here, interrogating him for hours about what he saw, maybe asking him to come down to the station to look through a book of photographs. And he thinks of his grandfather's gun.

'I'm sure somebody already has,' he says finally. 'We don't want to tie up the lines with redundant calls.'

After a moment's thought, Christopher nods.

'Probably right.'

'Poor girl, though. What if it had been Samantha?' He pauses, as if to think about that. 'We should move. Neighborhood's going downhill fast.'

Christopher looks away from him for a moment, seemingly lost in thought. He bites his lip. He looks down and scratches the web on his left hand between his thumb and index finger. Finally, he looks up.

'Do you really have a daughter?'

'What?'

Thomas can feel anger flushing his face, hot and itchy, but if Christopher notices, he hides it well – he just stares back, unflinching.

'Do you really have a daughter?' he says again. 'I see pictures around the apartment. And I know your stories. You've got plenty of stories: Samantha getting baptized even though you're not really religious because your wife insisted, Thanksgiving with the in-laws, all of that . . . but . . . I don't know. Maybe the stories don't quite add up, you know? Maybe . . . I just . . .' And with that – with it right out in the open – Christopher does break eye contact. 'I don't know. I'm sorry I said anything.'

Thomas doesn't know how to respond. He looks at Christopher and then looks away. He walks to the coffee table, picks up the picture there, and stares down at it for what seems to him like a very long time. He sets it down again.

'Does anyone else think I'm lying?' he asks finally. 'Doug? Larry, maybe?'

Christopher shrugs.

'I don't know. I don't think so. No one's said anything about it.'

Thomas picks the picture back up from the coffee table and looks at it for a while longer, and for some reason he feels like he's about to say goodbye to someone. It feels the same as it did when his mother left him standing on the lawn with a cardboard suitcase in his hand, left him standing next to grandma.

'Wave goodbye,' grandma said, and he did. He waved goodbye.

'I bought the first picture frame, this picture frame,' he says, holding it up, 'three years ago. It had a picture in it already – a picture of a woman and a little girl standing in front of the Golden Gate Bridge – so that you could imagine what your picture might look like inside the frame once you got it home and put it there. Only when I got the frame home, I had nothing to put in it, so I just set it on my coffee table and left the picture it came with inside. But sometimes, you know, when there was nothing on TV and I didn't feel like reading, I would, I don't know, just kind of look at that picture and wonder who that woman was. Was she nice? Did she smile easily at silly jokes? Was that little girl really her daughter? Did she get good grades in math? Maybe she could be my daughter too.' Thomas stops and simply looks at the picture a moment longer before he continues. 'About six months after I bought the first picture, I found another picture of the same woman. It was in a magazine, a cigarette advertisement. She was alone in that picture. I bought the magazine, and I took it home, and I cut her picture out and I framed it. After that, I guess I started hunting for them, pictures of the woman or the girl. Every time I left the house I hoped I would find one, and when I did, Jesus,' he lets out a melancholy chuckle, 'it was like,' he licks his lips, 'it was like running into an old friend.' He sets the picture back down again, collapses into the couch, and looks up at Christopher. 'Pretty pathetic, huh?'

'I don't think that's pathetic,' Christopher says.

'I do.' He scratches his cheek. 'I wish I had managed to pull the trigger before you came over. It would have saved me a lot of embarrassment.'

Christopher walks to the couch and sits down next to Thomas.

'Everybody lies,' he says.

Thomas shakes his head. 'People don't create entire families, wives and daughters, just so they have something to talk about when the guys at work start pulling pictures from their wallets. It's crazy. I know that. I don't know why I did it, exactly, but . . . I wish . . . I wish you hadn't . . .' and he trails off, looks down at his lap, and the room is silent.

After a long time, he says, 'I'm sorry.'

Christopher reaches out and puts a hand on Thomas's leg, just above the knee. Thomas looks at the hand for a moment and then looks up at Christopher.

'You don't have to apologize,' Christopher says.

'I don't think I started the lie to deceive anyone.'

'I know.'

'I'm sure I didn't start it to deceive anyone.'

'I know.'

'I started it for myself. I started it because I liked to pretend that I had something to come home to. Something more than a saucepan and a can of chili.' Thomas looks again, for just a moment, at the picture on the coffee table, and then he looks back at Christopher. 'No one cares about a mailman in his forties who drinks a six pack a night while watching *McHale's Navy*. People care about potential. They care about success. They don't care about failure. No one builds statues for the guy who never hurt anyone.'

'I care, Thomas,' Christopher says, and then he leans in to kiss him on the mouth, but Thomas pulls back and pushes Christopher's face away.

'What are you doing?' he says, a nervous tremor in his voice.

'I understand.'

Thomas shakes his head.

He's confused and he feels a knot tying itself in his stomach. But then Christopher reaches out gently and takes Thomas's chin in his hand and turns his head toward him, and Thomas looks into his eyes, and he'd be lying if he said he didn't like what he sees, and he'd be lying if he said he hasn't been lonesome, if he said he didn't want to feel close to someone – so when Christopher moves in for the second time to kiss him, Thomas lets him.

15

Patrick presses his thumb against the window lock as hard as he can, gritting his teeth and saying, 'Come on, you bitch,' under his breath, but the paint and rust don't want to give up their grip, and then, finally, they do, and the lock slides out of place in one quick jolt. His hand slips off of it and flies forward, and he punches the glass with an unformed fist, but the window doesn't break. He shakes his hand a moment, glances at the red indentation the lock put in the pad of his thumb, and then goes about pushing the window up. It takes some doing, but finally it slides upward in its wooden frame, groaning tiredly as it goes, like an old man getting out of bed on a winter morning.

Window up, Patrick pokes his head out into the cold night air and shouts, 'Hey. Leave that girl alone!'

The man standing over the girl looks up at him, pauses. For a moment Patrick thinks the guy's going to tell him to fuck off, to mind his own business, and for all Patrick knows this is a domestic dispute and he should fuck off. He can't really see clearly what's going on from here. If he hung his body out the window and looked straight down he'd be able to, but he's not gonna do that, and, anyway, it doesn't seem to be a simple domestic thing. Patrick and the man in the courtyard continue to look at each other. Then the man turns and runs away, out to the street, out into the shadows.

Patrick continues to look out into the courtyard for a moment. He watches the girl struggle to a sitting position. He can only see her knees and her head, her back half hidden by the apartment building and the shadows. But she seems to be okay. He pushes the window back down but continues to stand there looking through the glass, looking out at the other people standing in front of their windows.

Maybe, he thinks, he should call the police. He's sure someone already has, but maybe he should call them anyway, just in case. He walks to an end table and picks up the telephone, putting it to his ear.

'Patrick!'

He looks at the clock on the wall. It's only four thirty.

'I'll be right there, momma,' he says, and then sets the phone down in its cradle, wondering why she's calling him a half hour early.

He walks into the hallway to find out.

*

Patrick rolls the machine into the corner.

'No one said anything about it hurting,' he says.

'I'm not lying.'

'I didn't say you were. First thing in the morning, I'm gonna talk to Erin. You know you'll just get worse if we don't keep to the schedule.'

'I know, but it made my arm hurt.'

'Get some sleep, momma.'

He walks to the door and puts his hand on the light switch. Then he pauses, turns to his mother. Mom looks back at him through the folded flesh surrounding her eyes – they're like small lamps seen between nearly closed curtains – and frowns at something, the expression on his face he thinks.

'What is it, Pat?'

'It's Patrick, momma. No one calls me Pat anymore.'

'Not even your mother?'

Patrick shakes his head but regrets it when he sees that it's somehow hurt his mother's feelings.

'Well, what is it, Patrick?' she says finally.

He hesitates, considering how to tell his mother, and after he realizes there's no way to tell her but to tell her, he just comes out with it. 'I've been drafted,' he says. 'I'm supposed to report for my physical in the morning.'

Mom nods her understanding but she stays silent for a long time.

Finally, she says, 'How long have you known?'

'It doesn't matter.'

'If you're supposed to report tomorrow, you must have known for a while.'

'A little over a week.'

'Your mother is unwell. They might not make you go.'

'I've thought about that,' he says, and then finds himself looking at a cobweb in the corner.

'But,' mom says, waiting for the rest.

'I didn't say anything.'

'I know you didn't, but you're thinking something.'

Patrick opens his mouth to speak and then closes it again.

'I can't say it.'

'You want to go.'

After a moment, Patrick nods.

'I don't know if the Vietnamese are really so terrible,' he says, 'or if Communism is terrible, or anything like that. You know, I don't even read the newspaper, momma. I just . . . I want to experience something. I want to walk out the front door and see things I've never seen before and smell things I've never smelled before and . . . and maybe . . . maybe . . .' He stops, embarrassed with himself, maybe even a little bit ashamed of himself. He closes his eyes, swallows, opens his eyes, and looks at his mom. 'I'll report tomorrow, but I'll tell them you're sick,' he says. 'Maybe they won't make me go.'

'No,' mom says after a while. 'You should go.'

'But what about you?'

Mom smiles but it's an ugly thing. Her lips are dry and white. Her teeth are yellow. But it's a genuine smile, and it also lights up her eyes. It's the first time Patrick has seen a genuine smile on her face in a long time. He's not sure how something can be so ugly and beautiful at the same time, but there it is. Then, just as quickly, it's gone, and that's too bad; and Patrick will never know exactly what was going through her mind while that smile was in her eyes, and that's too bad, too.

'This isn't about me,' mom says.

'But, you said—'

'I was afraid. I've spent a long time being afraid. But you should go if that's what you want. I've stolen enough of your life, I guess.' And then she turns away, and simply looks at the far wall. She doesn't turn back.

Patrick opens his mouth to protest – to tell his mom that he won't go, that dad left them, and it hurt him in ways he can't explain, that he just can't do that to her – but stops before sound comes out. He stops because he thinks about what his life might be like if mom lives another ten years. Will he still be here, almost thirty, lifting her up and carrying her to the couch so that he can change her stinking sweat-stained sheets and apply salve to her bed sores? She'll only be seventy-two then. Lots of people live longer. Even sick people. The thought terrifies him.

He tells himself that if someone says it's all right, if

someone says you should go, well, that's not really leaving
– is it?

He just – he doesn't want to be here anymore.

'Okay, momma,' he says. 'Okay.'

He turns and walks out of the room.

16

Diane and Larry stand at the living-room window, looking out at the girl sitting in the courtyard. She's been sitting there for five minutes, just looking around. It must be cold out there. Diane wishes she'd get up and go inside. But more than that, she wishes Larry would stop lying to her.

'It's insulting,' she says.

'I'm not lying to you, Diane,' Larry says. 'You just want me to admit guilt because you've already convicted me in your head. You want me to admit guilt so you can say you knew it, you were right all along. Well, you're not right, Diane. I'm sorry, but you're not.'

Diane laughs, despite herself.

'You manipulative son of a bitch,' she says.

'Well, tell me it's not the truth, Diane.'

'It's not the truth, Larry,' she says.

'Then why don't you explain it to me? What the fuck is going through your head?'

'You want me to explain it to you?'

Larry nods. 'Yeah. Explain it to me, Diane, since you seem to have it all figured out.'

'You're goddamn right I have it all figured out. That's why I want you to admit guilt,' she says. 'I want you to admit guilt because when we had dinner with the Governses last week, Carol kept looking at me like she wanted to say something, like she felt sorry for me. Because you get home hours later than Thomas on bowling night. Because you don't seem interested in me at all anymore. But mostly,' she says, 'I want you to admit guilt because I can smell it on you. I can smell her on you. Every time you walk through that door afterwards, I can smell her, Larry. And your refusal to just admit what you've been doing is infuriating.'

She goes silent and looks at his eyes for a response.

He looks back at her and then he looks away. He looks to the corner and stares. He stares as if the answer to this situation might seep up through the carpet and reveal itself to him. When it doesn't, he turns back to Diane and looks at her silently.

She refuses to speak now. She's said what she has to say. She won't fill this silence for him, not even with the anger she is full of.

'I'm sorry.' He swallows.

'You're sorry?'

Larry nods.

'I'm sorry.'

'What are you sorry for?'

'You know what for.' He licks his lips. 'Are you really gonna make me say it?'

Diane nods.

'You did it,' she says. 'You can damn well say it.'

'I'm sorry,' he begins, and he does seem to be having a hard time getting it out. 'I'm sorry that I cheated on you, Diane. I'm so sorry,' he says, and now tears are standing out in his eyes, but it's too late for that. She's shut off the part of herself capable of feeling sympathy for him. What she feels now is rage and coldness.

'Who is she?'

'It doesn't matter.'

'Of course it matters,' she says. 'Of course it matters.'

'But it doesn't, Diane. It doesn't matter. It was a mistake.'

'A *mistake*? You left her bed an hour ago.'

Larry doesn't respond. He stands silently, looking at her, and then he drops his gaze.

'How long has it been going on?'

'Jesus, Diane,' he says, 'I don't—'

'How fucking long?'

Larry looks to the corner again.

'I don't know,' he says. 'Six months, maybe.'

Diane clenches her jaw and says through gritted teeth, 'You son of a bitch.'

She looks around for something to throw or hit or something and what her hand falls upon is a porcelain horse – a stupid fucking porcelain horse – another gift from Larry's senile old bag of a mother; she must just sit around all day looking at catalogs and ordering useless crap, which she then pawns off on relatives. Larry must know what's going to happen next because he backs away quickly and shields himself. Diane raises the porcelain horse above her head and lets it fly. She throws it as hard as she can. It shoots straight through the air, spinning as it goes, head first, then tail, then head, in a straight line, no arc at all, aimed right for Larry's cheating fucking face, but he ducks, and it shatters on the wall behind him, scarring the paint, exploding, a few pieces of the porcelain embedding themselves in the plaster.

'Six months isn't a mistake,' she shouts. 'One time is a mistake. Six months is a relationship!'

'I'm sorry,' Larry says again, in a tone that makes Diane want to throw something else. And this time she wouldn't miss. She doesn't throw anything, though. She only speaks.

'That's not good enough,' she says.

Then she turns away, silently, and walks down the hallway toward the bedroom. She had hoped when she laid out all her suspicions that he would somehow have an explanation that she couldn't think of, an explanation that evaporated all her suspicions and worries and fears. Even till the last second she hoped that. But once it was out of her mouth and she saw the look on his face she knew. She'd been right and there was no harmless explanation, no matter how badly she wanted for there to be one. There was only the truth.

'Where are you going?' Larry says.

'To pack my things.'

17

Peter sits on the couch beside his wife. Bettie sits on the other side of Anne, swishing white wine around in a red wine glass and watching it. Then she puts the glass to her mouth and swallows the last of it, leaving a film of lipstick on the rim.

Ron stands at the living-room window, looking out.

Peter wonders what Anne would do if he decided to leave her for Bettie. He wonders what Ron would do. Ron is the kind of man who claims he wouldn't be upset by such a thing – if a woman decides to leave, well, that's just the way it is; there are others – but Peter suspects his feelings are a bit more complex than that. He wonders if Bettie would consider leaving Ron. There were moments they shared that seemed like more than just sex to him, that seemed important somehow.

He wonders if anyone would notice him missing if he

left for just a couple minutes so he could clean the whiskey out of the carpet.

'She's just sitting there,' Ron says. 'She might be hurt. I think I see blood. Maybe we should call the police.'

Anne says, 'I'm sure someone already has. We shouldn't tie up the lines.'

Peter can see half a dozen faces in their windows from where he's sitting on the couch – silhouettes looking out into the night, looking past the night and into other people's apartments like he's looking into theirs – and he imagines that Anne is right.

Ron must, too, because he says, 'True enough.'

So, Peter thinks, at least that's settled.

Ron wanders to the kitchen. 'I'm gonna fix myself a drink,' he says. 'Vodka tonic. Anyone else want anything?'

Ron is almost two inches taller than Peter, and though he's a desk jockey same as Peter is, the man intimidates him. He looks like he can take a punch, doesn't seem like he'd be helpless if his car broke down on the side of the road, probably enjoys fishing and hunting and camping.

'There's a bottle of white wine in the fridge,' Anne says. 'I'd like a glass of that.'

'Is that what I was drinking?' Bettie asks.

Anne nods.

'Me too,' Bettie calls to her husband. 'But I already have a glass.'

Peter stands.

'I'll take it in there. I could use a refill myself.'

He takes the glass from her, making sure he brushes his fingers across the back of her hand, and then he tries to grab his own tumbler from the cork coaster on the table, but the coaster sticks to bottom of the glass with a water bond, and he can't shake the damned thing off.

Finally, smiling, Anne reaches forward and pulls the coaster off the glass and sets it back down on the table.

'Thanks, hon',' Peter says, and heads to the kitchen with the wine glass and the tumbler.

When he gets there he finds Ron randomly opening and closing cupboards, looking for glasses, but finding spices, canned goods, pastas, cereals.

'On the left,' Peter says.

'That's where I was gonna check next,' Ron says, opening the cupboard, pulling out two tumblers.

'I still have my glass,' Peter says.

Ron glances at him and says, 'So you do,' puts one tumbler back, and grabs a wine glass in its place. 'For Anne.'

Peter walks to the freezer and gets out two handfuls of ice, dropping them in the tumblers.

There is a row of liquor laid out on the yellow tiled counter and Ron goes about mixing his vodka tonic and pouring Peter his whiskey. 'Water?'

'Yeah, about half.'

Ron nods.

'How many times,' Peter says, shutting the freezer and opening the fridge, 'how many times have you and Bettie . . . uh . . .'

'Swapped?' Ron asks, raising a thick black eyebrow.

Peter nods, then goes about scanning the fridge for the white wine Anne claimed was in here, but he doesn't see it.

'I don't know,' Ron says. 'Half a dozen or so.'

'Honey,' Peter calls.

'It's in the door, on the bottom shelf, by the ketchup,' Anne calls back before Peter has a chance to ask his question.

He looks in the door, on the bottom shelf, by the ketchup, and there it is.

'Thank you.'

'You're welcome.'

'Did you ever fall for one of the girls,' Peter says. 'Did you ever fall for one of the girls you . . . you know?'

'Fucked?'

'Fucked,' Peter says, feeling slightly embarrassed.

He pulls the cork from the wine bottle and splits what's left between the two waiting glasses.

'I love Bettie,' Ron says. 'Swapping doesn't make me love her less. In a way,' he says, 'it makes me love her more. I mean, I'm not gonna lie to you, sex with other women is fun, it's a nice change of pace, it's exciting, but you know what's really exciting? Making love with my wife afterwards. Knowing that even though another man has had her, she's still mine. Proving she's mine by . . .' Ron smiles. 'You've never had an orgasm like the one you'll have with Anne once me and Bettie leave,' Ron says. 'I promise you that. There's something about the sex right after . . .' He shakes his head, still smiling. Then he hands Peter his whiskey. 'Cheers,' he says.

Peter raises his whiskey and they tap glasses.

'Cheers.'

Peter drains his and pours himself another.

Ron laughs.

'I guess you worked up a thirst.'

'Something like that,' Peter says.

Then each of them grabs a glass of white wine from the counter and they head out to the living room where their women await them.

Peter walks to the ladies sitting on the couch and hands a glass of wine to Bettie.

'Here you go.'

'Thank you,' Bettie says, smiling.

But Ron isn't smiling, not anymore. He stands in the middle of the living room, unmoving.

'That was for Anne,' he says.

'There's two glasses of wine,' Peter says, realizing that he's made a mistake – he knew he made a mistake, in fact, since the second he held the glass out to Bettie and saw Anne reach for it, then pull back, a hurt expression passing quickly across her face – but defending himself all the same, 'does it matter who gets which?'

'No,' Ron says.

'All right, then.'

'Except why wouldn't you hand it to your wife?'

'Bettie was closer.'

'They're sitting right next to each other!'

'Why are you making a thing out of this?'

'Because,' Ron says, 'it just dawned on me what you were saying in the kitchen.'

Anne looks from Ron to Peter, her eyes shining with questions, but she doesn't ask Peter anything. Instead, she turns back to Ron.

'What,' she says, 'was he saying in the kitchen?'

'Honey,' Peter says.

'I'd like to know, too,' Bettie says before sipping her wine.

Peter looks from Ron to Anne to Bettie. He feels trapped. How did this happen? All he did was hand a glass of wine to the wrong person.

'I didn't say anything,' he says.

'Apparently you did,' Anne says.

'You're not in love with my wife,' Ron says.

'You told him you were in love with Bettie?'

'No.'

'Peter,' Ron says, 'you're not.'

'I didn't.'

'Peter.'

'I . . .'

He feels lost.

'Trust me,' Ron says.

'I . . .'

'How long have you and Anne been together?'

Peter is too flustered to answer. He still doesn't know

how this happened. Forty-five minutes ago he was thinking this was one of the best nights of his life, and now he's standing here surrounded – feeling surrounded, anyway – thinking the night might well be going in the opposite direction, thinking it's well on its way.

'Ten years,' Anne says. Then she looks to Peter. 'We've been together for ten years.'

'I . . .' He looks at Anne. 'I know that,' he says, finally able to get words out in sentence form. 'I know we've been together for ten years. We met on Valentine's Day, 1954. I know that.'

But Anne only looks away.

'I knew this was a bad idea,' she says. 'I don't know why I let you talk me into it.'

'Ten years,' Ron says. 'And how long was it before you knew you loved her?'

'Why are you interrogating me?'

'I'm not. I'm trying to make a point.'

'Then make your fucking point and stop asking me questions.'

'I'm almost there. How long before you knew you loved Anne?'

'I don't know,' Peter says. 'Four or five months.'

'You've known me, what,' Ron says, 'a year? You talked to Bettie twice in that time, both times at work functions. You don't fall in love with someone like that.'

Peter looks to Anne. Her eyes are welling with tears,

welling and about to overflow with them, and goddamn it, he does not want to see that.

'Anne,' he says, 'I didn't tell Ron I was in love with Bettie.'

'Sex can confuse people,' Ron says.

'I didn't tell Ron that I was in love with Bettie,' he says again, as if that will be enough to make everything better.

'But you're not saying you're not,' Anne says, and the tears finally overflow and roll down her cheeks.

Peter only looks back at her, not knowing what to say. He does not want to see this. He does not want this to be happening.

'Peter?' Anne says.

'Sex can make people think things that aren't true,' Ron says. 'Don't let this confuse things between you and your wife.'

'Will you shut the fuck up? This was your fucking idea,' Peter says, turning and glaring at Ron. 'It was your fucking idea.'

'I thought you could handle it.'

'You wanted to fuck my wife,' Peter says. 'That's what you thought. You saw my wife and you thought, I'd like to fuck her. That's all there was to it. You thought I could handle it? Fuck you.'

'And you didn't want to fuck my wife?'

'Say you're not in love with Bettie,' Anne says. 'Just say it, Peter.'

Peter swallows. 'I'm sorry, Anne. It's just . . . and I'm sorry, Ron . . . it's, Bettie and I, we . . . we shared . . .'

'Peter,' Bettie says.

'What?'

He turns to look at her, feeling his stomach drop with fear, suddenly remembering that another person is here who has a say in this – whatever this is.

She shakes her head.

'What?' he says again.

'We shared sex,' she says. 'That's it.'

He licks his lips. Oh, God.

'But – but you don't understand,' he says.

'It was sex,' she says. 'That's it. That was the point.'

'You're lying,' he says. 'You're lying to spare Ron's feelings.'

'No.' She shakes her head.

'Oh, goddamn it,' Anne says.

'But—' Peter turns back to Ron. 'This was your fucking idea.'

'But it was your mistake,' Ron says.

'I can't believe I was stupid enough to let you talk me into this.'

Anne gets to her feet and disappears into the dark hallway.

A moment later, there is the slam of a door.

Peter walks to the couch and falls into it.

He puts his head into his hands.

'Fuck,' he says. 'Fuck.'

18

'Um. Let's see,' David White says, looking through the glass front of a case which holds dozens of donuts. He ate before he started his shift but he's hungry again.

'Take your time,' the cop standing behind him says. 'It's not like anyone's waiting.'

Then there's a yelp of sirens and a brief flash of light from the ambulance on the other side of the window. He probably shouldn't be stuffing himself with donuts any-way.

'Guess that's it,' he says. 'How much?'

'On the house,' the man behind the counter says. 'Go save some lives.'

'Thanks,' David says. ''Preciate it.'

Then he turns away and heads for the front door, kick-ing it open since his hands are full, and then slipping through before it has a chance to swing shut. As he nears the ambulance, John reaches over the width of the cab and shoves open the passenger's door for him.

'Thanks,' he says, getting into the ambulance, handing John his coffee, pulling shut his door. 'What do we got?'

'Car accident,' John says.

David nods, tries to take a sip of his coffee, but just as the cup touches his lip, John puts the ambulance in gear, it lurches forward, and coffee spills down the front of David's uniform.

'Shit.'

John glances over. 'Sorry.'

David nods but waits until the ambulance is up to speed before attempting a second sip.

He looks out the window at the blur of night as they head toward whatever carnage awaits them. He is tired. He is always tired. He just can't seem to sleep. Part of it, he thinks, is this job. The graveyard shift is a brutal shift no matter how long you've been working it. He gets off work and drives home in a half-dream, exhausted, at a time when the day is just beginning to gain speed. The sun is up, evaporating the last of the midnight dew. People are showering and shaving and eating eggs and driving to work and he is headed in the opposite direction toward home. But not toward bed. Never toward bed – not immediately. The noise – of traffic and talking and life – keeps him awake. He pushes through the front door and walks straight to his couch and sits down. His dog Sarah greets him, licks his hand, curls up against his leg, and he pets her absently. For the next hour or two, he stares. That's all. He simply stares at his reflection in the gray television screen, stares at the wall, stares at his waking dreams in the corners of the room. Sometimes he talks to Sarah. Sometimes he tells her about his night. 'Tonight was rough,' he'll say. 'Got called to a shooting. Man was shot in the head, directly between the eyes, but he didn't die. So the gunman shot him again and ran, but he still didn't die. When we pulled up, he was sitting on the curb. Just sitting there. Arms resting on his knees. He looked at us and smiled. Raised an arm in greeting. "Hello," he said. If it wasn't for the two dots on his forehead, he could have been anybody. Two red dots. One right in the middle of the forehead, the other above his left eyebrow. They were both oozing a little bit of blood, but they weren't bleeding bad. Just big enough to poke a finger into. For a minute, I thought, this is one tough motherfucker. He took two bullets to the brain and doesn't seem phased. Then I saw the back of his head. The exit wounds were big enough to shove baseballs into. Tangerines, anyway. Then I saw ten feet to his left where most of the contents of his head had splattered. He was just a zombie. "How you doing, sir?" I said. "Hello," he said again. Just a zombie, Sarah. That's all. And he wouldn't die. We got him to the hospital. He could have walked, but we didn't let him. We rolled him into the emergency room, and every time he saw someone he would say it. "Hello. Hello. Hello. Hello." It was unnerving. Doctors say he'll probably be dead by the end of the week if he's actually gonna go – but he may live.

If he's not dead by then, he'll probably live. They're cleaning up the wounds as if he's gonna live. If he does, he'll just be able to walk around and say "Hello." He'll just be a zombie with half a head. "Hello. Hello. Hello. Hello." I asked a friend of mine who's a cop if there's any leads. He seems to think they'll never catch the guy who did it. No one's talking. Even the woman who called the police, she says she only heard the shots. The first one, she just thought it was car backfire or something. By the time she got to the window after the second shot, the shooter was gone, leaving behind the zombie, leaving behind this guy with a wife and a daughter, this guy who can walk and say "Hello" but can't do nothing else.' Sometimes he'll talk to Sarah and sometimes he'll just sit and stare. But he never sleeps when he gets home. Around ten o'clock in the morning, once everyone who's going to work has gone, it's a bit quieter and he's had time to flush work from his body – it's drained down and leaked from the soles of his feet – so he walks to the bedroom and lays himself on the bed and stares at his closet door. After a while, he gets up and opens it. David does not like closed doors. He doesn't know why, but he doesn't. He hates not being able to see exactly what's on the other side. When he moves into an apartment, the first thing he does is get out a screwdriver and a hammer and start removing hinge-pins and the doors that separate rooms. He leaves on the closet door and the bathroom door. Closets sometimes get cluttered, and though he almost never has company, the bathroom door is necessary when he does. But he can't sleep with the closet door closed. So he opens it – even though it means Sarah may run off with a shoe – then he walks back to bed and lays down again. Around eleven he'll finally get to sleep. But by two or three, the heat will wake him up, the heat and the afternoon sunlight, and he'll be up for good. The rest of the day he'll just spend wandering around, a zombie himself, grocery shopping, doing laundry, vacuuming the carpet, washing the dishes he's let pile up in the sink. Sometimes he goes to a massage parlor. He always feels guilty about it afterwards – those girls who don't speak English and have few other options – but he does it anyway. Sometimes he just needs to get it out of his system, to have physical contact with another human being, physical contact of any kind.

And then, eventually, it's time for work again.

There are already two police cars parked on the side of the road with their lights flashing when David and John arrive in their ambulance. Flares blaze, and one uniformed cop who David doesn't recognize is standing in the street to make sure looky loos keep their distance. David can't imagine there've been too many at this time of night – but who knows?

John parks the ambulance on the wrong side of the street, in front of one of the police cars, killing the sirens while the lights continue to bleed the night.

'Looks pretty ugly,' he says.

David nods in agreement, and then pushes open his door and steps outside. He walks toward the upended Fiat and looks inside through the bloody side window. The car is empty.

'He's over there,' the policeman he doesn't recognize says.

David looks up and sees the guy pointing to his right. He follows the finger to a storefront with a shattered window. Behind the shattered glass, David can see several fallen bicycles and flashlight beams shifting around, crossing one another. Other cops, he assumes.

'Inside,' the cop says. 'He's unconscious.'

David nods and walks back to the ambulance.

He grabs a scoop stretcher from the back and heads toward the building. John follows.

'Son of a bitch,' David says. 'You son of a bitch.'

He stares down at Mr. Vacanti lying unconscious behind the counter of this night-dark bicycle shop. He's flat on his back, one arm folded underneath his body, the other angled up, bent at the elbow, touching the top of his head with the thumb, shaping the number four. There is a six-inch shard of glass jutting from his forehead, a shelf of glass, and he's lying in a pool of his own blood.

For a brief moment – just for a second – David considers simply reaching down and twisting that shard of glass, shoving it in further, as far as he can, until it hits bone on the other side, at the back of the head, and then giving it one last push, till it scars the vinyl floor beneath. He thinks there'd be a sense of satisfaction as he felt the spongy brain being sliced through, as he heard the pop of bone giving way.

'What is it?' John says behind him.

'What?' David says.

'You said, "son of a bitch,"' John says. And then, after a moment, when he doesn't reply, 'David?'

'What?'

'What is it?'

'Oh,' David says. 'I know him.'

'Who is he?'

'Just someone I know,' David says. 'Someone I used to know. Let's get him into the ambulance.'

19

Kat doesn't know how long she's been out here, she doesn't know how long ago the man with the knife left, but she knows she has to do something. She can't just sit here forever. She can't just sit here and bleed.

For a while, though, she doesn't know what else to do. There's something wrong with her head. She can't think. Why can't she think?

There's a bench there, not ten feet away. She can get to the bench. She's almost sure of it. Anybody could get to the bench. It's right there, not ten feet away.

She can get there; she knows she can.

She gets on hands and knees and starts crawling in that direction.

Her fingers are very cold. Her nose is very cold. Her lips are very cold, and when she licks them, because they're dry, dry and cracked, she can barely feel them. It's almost like they're not her own. Somehow, it reminds her of when she was a little girl. She used to love to ride her bike. She would ride as fast as she could, and then stop pedaling, and just coast as long as she could, smiling away, the cold and wild wind rushing against her, freezing her knuckles and her nose and her lips, but she didn't care because she was flying.

Flying.

A brief smile touches her cold, cracked lips as that memory passes through her head, but it's quickly gone.

Every thought that enters her head is quickly gone. She can't think. The pain overwhelms. Every time she moves at all, the pain seems to be the only part of the world that's completely real. Her right side, inside her body, under her armpit – that's where it's the worst. It itches. It feels like it's frozen and on fire simultaneously. And it itches.

All she wanted was a gee-dee bath.

She doesn't understand what happened. Why did that man stab her? She had never seen him before and she didn't do anything to him so why did he stab her? She's sure she never saw him before tonight.

She reaches the bench and puts her arms against the seat of it and pushes herself up. The paint has been worn away by weather and the seats of jeans and she can feel the coarse grain of the gray wood beneath her arms. She hears herself groan as she lifts herself, as she straightens herself out, and she feels more warm, coppery-smelling blood pouring down her back, and jabbing pain in her armpit, and the groan turns to a scream, but she doesn't stop pushing herself up. She doesn't stop until she's pushed herself to her feet. It feels precarious, but here she is, standing. She feels herself swaying left, then right. Black out-of-focus dots dance in front of her eyes, moving this way and that, like insects, like dust motes in a beam of light. She feels dizzy, but she's standing – she's standing.

She can feel something warm running down the front of her now, too, and she remembers the second attack, and she looks down at herself, and she sees four more holes in the front of her dress, her light blue dress, her new dress that she got from Woolworth's only a week ago, a treat from her to herself for working so hard last month. She'd gotten some compliments on it earlier tonight and she was glad she bought it.

She looks around. Most of the faces that were looking down on her before are gone. Most of the living-room lights have turned off. But a few living rooms are still lit up, and in others, even with the lights off, she can see people standing behind the glass, looking at her. Maybe they turned off their lights to get a completely unobstructed view, maybe not; either way, a few faces with white eyes still look down on her.

'Help . . . me,' she says. 'Please.'

She meant for it to be a shout, but it's barely a whisper. A weak breeze. A rustling of leaves. She has strength for very little more than that – but she tries.

'Someone,' she says, her voice breaking, 'help! Please!'

She hears desperation in her own voice.

The people standing in their living rooms watching her do not move.

Maybe this is just a nightmare. It feels like it must be nothing more than that. It feels like that's what it has to be. When she was a teenager, Kat used to lie in bed, wondering if her whole life was nothing but a dream. She would lie in bed and she would be afraid to go to sleep because she thought when she woke up she would be waking into her real life and in her real life she was an old woman already – or something like that. So she would lie in bed, thinking this life was a dream, but it was a good dream, a dream she didn't want to wake from, in part simply because she didn't know what she'd be waking to – what was reality? – but now she wishes this were a dream. She hopes it's a dream. No matter what she wakes to, it has to be better than this. She closes her eyes and wills herself to wake up, but when she opens them again, she's still here, surrounded by concrete and glass, the courtyard empty but for her.

Why isn't anyone helping her? If this isn't a dream, why isn't anyone helping her?

Because it's a nightmare, a voice says.

Tears stream down her pale face.

She can't feel them, but she knows they're there.

And for a moment she allows herself to just let go. To cry. Her body shakes with the crying, convulses with it, and the convulsions send sharp pain shooting into her, send more blood seeping out of her, but she allows herself to cry anyway because she knows it's coming whether she wants it to or not.

Then she makes it stop. She simply shuts it off. She can't allow herself to bleed to death out here. She can't allow that. She has to do something. She has to get inside, that's what she has to do, and crying won't get her there.

She looks in the direction of her apartment, the direction from which she crawled. Her eyes follow the trail of blood leading around the corner. So much blood. It looks brown under the courtyard's light, brown instead of red.

Where is her purse?

On the front porch. She dropped it on the front porch.

Where are her keys? She closes her eyes, trying to think.

They're in the door, but she doesn't need them. The door is open. She remembers opening the door, so the door has to be open.

Sometimes, when it's hot outside and she wants to let a breeze blow through the apartment, she keeps the door open so the wind can blow in through it and out through the window. She insisted on getting one of the complex's eight garden apartments for just that reason. She has to prop it open, though, because sometimes the wind blows the door shut again. But that didn't happen this time. She would have heard the door slamming if it had. That means the door is open.

All she has to do is get there.

An attainable goal.

Easy-peasy.

She can see herself doing it. She just walks to the door one step at a time. She's dizzy and it's not easy to stay on her feet, but she holds her arms out, away from her body, to keep her balance – the way she did when she was a little girl and trying to walk along something narrow like that short wall that surrounded the shrubbery in front of her grade school; she would pretend she was a high-wire act in a circus and she was world-famous and she would close her eyes and hold her arms out, away from her body for balance – and she walks, one step at a time, and then she can see it, her front door, open not closed because she would have heard it slam if it was closed, and she just has to put her arms forward and push it the rest of the way open, and so she does that, and then she's inside, and there's her couch and her favorite chair and the throw pillows she bought a couple months ago that match the curtains and the pictures of her family, and the phone, there's her phone, and she walks straight to it on the end table in her living room and she picks it up and she puts it to her ear and she says, Hello, operator . . .

'Hello, operator,' she says, still standing in the courtyard, her body swaying in the night air. 'Hello, I've been . . . stabbed. I need an ambulance.'

Yes, she thinks. That's what she'll do.

It's an attainable goal.

Like pouring a drink. Like changing a tire.

Easy-peasy.

She concentrates only on what she's doing, and she

takes her first step toward her apartment. Her left knee wants to buckle as she moves her right leg forward, but she manages to keep it locked in place – shakily, true, but it holds – and then she puts her right foot down. That's one step. She's one step closer to being saved, one step closer to saving herself. She locks her right knee and drags her left leg up even with her right leg. She stands, breathing hard. Okay, she thinks. Again. She puts her left leg forward, carefully, carefully . . . but then, suddenly, without warning, her right leg gives up, just quits, I'm done, and that's it, there's nothing under her but ground, and she simply breaks into pieces and crumbles to the concrete surface beneath her.

'Fuck,' she says as she falls, the first time she's said an out-loud curse in a very long time, but she doesn't care anymore. She just doesn't fucking care.

She slaps the concrete with the palm of her hand, and this time when the tears come, she doesn't try to stop them at all.

20

Alan pulls his police cruiser to the curb in front of a small one-story house – near the corner of a one-way street where brownstone row houses give way to single-family Tudor-style homes with lots of dark half-timbering – and kills the engine. The front lights are on but the curtains are closed. The curtains are red, so the light splashing out through them and onto the lawn is red, too. Alan thinks the red curtains mean the guy's either married or a fag, and Alan is guessing married – a fag wouldn't have the stones to pull something like this.

He pushes his way out of the car and walks around to the trunk. He pops the trunk and takes care of a couple things that need taking care of. Then he slams it shut and walks across the dewy lawn to the front door of the house. The door is white with a ridiculously large gold knocker on it, just below a peephole.

Alan knocks on the door with his fist, then stands with his hands behind his back and waits.

Only a few seconds later the door is pulled open by a fat man in his late thirties or early forties, reddish hair, ruddy face. His name is Todd Reynolds. Charlie told him that. Charlie also told him that the man had no prior convictions, not even a speeding ticket. Model citizen.

Model asshole, if you ask Alan.

'You made it,' Mr. Reynolds says in a voice that sounds like it's coming from just behind his nose and just above the roof of his mouth – thick and nasally, almost cartoonish. He smiles.

'I made it,' Alan agrees.

'Good, good.'

'You know, Mr. Reynolds—'

'Todd.'

'You know, Todd,' Alan says, 'I don't want to tell you how to do business, but I gotta say, it's not the smartest thing in the world, inviting a man you're trying to extort to your home in the dead-dark hours of the night. Bad things can happen to a man at night. And according to recent statistics,' he says, 'eighty-seven percent of people who are murdered are murdered in their own homes.' He smiles. 'Your wife and kids in bed?'

'Who says I have a wife and kids?'

'You're wearing a wedding ring and I saw a baseball bat on the lawn when I walked up here. Wife,' he says, nodding at the wedding ring, 'kid,' he says, nodding toward the lawn.

'Goddamn it,' Todd says. 'I told that little bastard not to leave shit laying around.'

'Kids,' Alan says.

'Indeed,' Todd says. 'But to the point. You can't frighten me, Officer Kees, if that's what you're trying to do with your talk of murder. If I come forward, not only will you no longer have a career, but there's a chance you'll do jail time; and we all know what happens to cops in prison. And the truth is, I don't want that. All I want is a cut. Five thousand dollars. By tomorrow. I already told your friend, but he insisted on sending you here tonight for some reason.'

'He wanted me to try to talk sense to you.'

'My decision is made,' Todd says. 'I'm not negotiating.'

Alan nods.

'You're not negotiating and I can't frighten you. Is that about how it is?'

'That's about how it is.'

'Then you're dumber than I thought.'

Todd smiles. 'Why's that, Officer Kees?'

Alan lets his arms drop to his sides, revealing gloved fists. In the right hand, a rusty tire iron.

'Take a look at the man standing in front of you. Do I frighten you now?'

Todd's smile – the one that says he's won and he knows it – vanishes.

'Wait a minute,' he says, taking a step back across the foyer's gray tile.

'Charlie thought you might be reasonable,' Alan says, 'but as soon as I heard you wanted five grand, which, by the way, is fourteen hundred more than Charlie and I have collected combined, I knew better. I knew you were beyond reason.'

'Please,' Todd says.

'Now, I'm a good police officer, Mr. Reynolds. *Todd*. Given the current situation, I can understand your not believing me, but it's true. I am. But here's a fact you might not be aware of – cops put their lives in danger every day of the week, and for that we are paid a pittance. I found a way to make a little extra money. I have a new wife at home, Todd, with a bun in the oven. I want to give my wife and child the kind of life they deserve, the same kind of life you want to give your family. Now maybe the way I found to make that extra money isn't legal, but you'll be the first person it's hurt – just about the first person, anyway – and that's because you're threatening my family, Todd.'

'Now, hold on,' Todd says. 'Hold on a minute. We can still work this—'

'And when people threaten my family,' Alan says, ignoring Todd completely, 'when people threaten to destroy my family, that forces me into the position of having to destroy them. It's not something I enjoy doing, Todd. It's something I have to do. It's something you've made me do. You've forced my hand, Todd – that's all there is to it.'

And then the tire iron in Alan's fist is whistling through the cold night air. There's the sound of something hard and unforgiving smashing into something soft and hollow. Blood splatters the white front door, paints the gold knocker red. Todd whips around, his jaw hanging like a door with a broken hinge. He spins in a full circle before he hits the ground. He looks up at Alan. The lower half of his face is carnage, the face of a feasting lion, only the blood is his own.

'Please,' he says through swollen jaw and destroyed mouth, flakes of teeth falling out of it like crumbs, hanging from blood and spittle on his chin, falling to his shirt.

'No,' Alan says.

Todd reaches for Alan's leg, but he's slow, and Alan steps aside easily.

Then swings the tire iron again, swings it straight down as if he were chopping a cord of wood and this was his final piece. There is a wet sound when the tire iron makes contact, a sound like a melon breaking open and spilling its sweet contents.

That sound is followed by silence.

Alan hopes it remains silent. He hopes that Todd's family is accustomed to his late nights, hopes they've learned to sleep through whatever noise he's in the habit of making. He would hate for them to have to meet the same fate, but he'll do what he has to. Read the Old Testament: sometimes the sins of the father are paid for by the son: God takes His pound of flesh from whomever He can.

Alan simply stands and listens for a long moment.

Blood drips from the clawed end of the tire iron in his hand.

After a minute has passed, Alan is satisfied. He steps over Todd and into the house, tracking Todd's blood past the tile foyer and onto an area rug.

'Fuck,' he whispers under his breath.

He smears the blood he tracked onto the carpet so no one will be able to tell shoe size or type. Then he walks to the television sitting in the corner of the room, unplugs it, and hefts it up. It's a heavy son of a bitch, but at least it's not one of those enormous oak models; those things weigh a hundred pounds or more. He carries it outside and to his car – cord dragging behind him – and sets it down by the sidewalk, on a narrow strip of dead grass there. Then he walks to the trunk, opens it, and puts the tire iron back inside. Next, he opens the back door of the cruiser and hefts the TV into the passenger's seat.

'You're under arrest,' he tells it, smiling to himself, and then slams the door shut on it.

With that part done, he walks back up across the lawn – past a child's baseball bat – and back into the Reynolds house. He scans the living room, looking for a phone, and finally sees it, hanging on the wall by the doorway to the kitchen. He picks it up to dial, then stops. He hangs it up. Not yet, he thinks. Film first, then phone.

If I were 8mm film, he thinks, where would I be? He scans the living room, not seeing any decent hiding places, then walks into the kitchen and – as quietly as possible – opens several cupboards and drawers but sees nothing. He doesn't even know whether the guy had the film developed or not. Maybe it's already been developed and is sitting on a spool somewhere waiting to be watched; or maybe it's just a small can of undeveloped celluloid tape. No, it's been developed. Maybe he developed it himself in a bucket, but it's been developed. This was a man who was certain of what he had – so certain he'd probably watched it over and over again projected onto the concrete wall in his basement.

Basement.

Alan only takes a minute to find the door, and then he trudges his way downstairs. The light switch is on the wall at the bottom of the stairs – that way you can kill yourself trying to get to it in the dark, he thinks – and he flips it and a naked bulb hanging from a frayed brown wire comes to life, illuminating the room. There are cans of paint stacked in a corner, various colors running down their sides; baskets of laundry nearby, overflowing with dainties; boxes labeled *Xmas*. And there's a projector on a small card table surrounded by several spools of film. One spool of film is already loaded onto it, and it's aimed, just as Alan thought, at a concrete wall.

The part of the wall it's aimed at has been painted white, runny and uneven.

Alan walks to the projector, turns it on; a rectangle of white light splashes onto the wall.

Alan plays the film, the projector adding a familiar clicking soundtrack to the proceedings. It was shot through a window. The colors are strange, greenish and dull, and the film is very scratchy, so Alan suspects that Mr. Reynolds – *Todd* – did, in fact, develop it in a bucket down here rather than have it professionally done. Maybe he wanted to keep its subject-matter to himself. He imagines hundreds of amateur pornographers have done the same thing with their films. Despite the discoloration and the scratches, it's obvious what's going on. There's Alan and Charlie stepping from a vehicle, meeting another man, Big Fish, who is walking – limping: Alan really laid on the charm – out the front door of a brownstone. Big Fish pulls a white envelope out of his inside jacket pocket and hands it to Alan. Alan opens the envelope, thumbs through money, nods, and he and Charlie walk away, walk back to the car. The film continues, jittery and handheld, as Alan and Charlie start the car, as the car drives away, as Big Fish stands and watches till Alan and Charlie are out of sight, as he flips them the bird once he's sure they can't see, as he turns and heads back into the brownstone – but the important part is the hand-off. Then there's a cut, flickering white overexposed frames, and then a picture again. Front of the same brownstone. Big Fish is handing something that's not money off to some spic, a big manila envelope that he shows is full of small bags. The spic takes a bag at random and sticks a pinky into it and tastes it, then he nods. The two talk. Then they separate, both walking out of the picture. The camera shakes and turns around and an out-of-focus Todd gives it a grin and a thumbs up. Then the film ends with some more flashing white frames, and then blackness.

Alan grabs the spool of film and heads back upstairs.

Upstairs, by the kitchen, he picks up the phone a second time.

'Hello,' he whispers into the phone, not wanting to wake the family, 'I need the police. It's an emergency.'

He tells the police his name is Todd Reynolds. He tells them someone is trying to break into his house, a Negro man is trying to break into his house. He tells them the address. He says, 'He's coming in! He's coming—' and he hangs up the telephone quickly, smiling to himself.

That was perfect. He should have been an actor. He could play a policeman on TV. The pay would certainly be better.

He walks back out into the night, careful to step over the gathering pool of blood this time. The last thing he wants is to slip and fall at this stage in the night. He peels off the rubber gloves as he walks toward his police cruiser. His hands are wet with sweat and his fingers have already begun to prune. He'll have to put the gloves back on one more time before the night is finished, but until then, he wants to give them a chance to breathe.

21

William pulls the long station wagon into the driveway, parking it over a metal tray lined with sand. The car's been leaking oil lately but he hasn't had time to get it fixed. A tray to collect the oil is the best he can do for now.

He sits behind the wheel and stares at the white garage door. It is dented where he pulled in too far about three months ago and tapped it. It's also beginning to rust inside the dent, where the pinching of metal caused the paint to crack. Another thing that needs fixing.

And now he's got blood on his work boots.

And maybe someone will be able to identify him.

At least he left when he did. The police are probably there right now, so it's good he left when he did.

He pushes the station wagon's door open and steps out. He looks at his boots in the moon's light. The blood looks almost black out here, and there is a lot of it, but he might be able to scrub it out. He hopes so. They're almost new and he would hate to have to replace them already. He just broke them in.

He should have known better than to wear them tonight. But then, he wasn't thinking clearly; he wasn't thinking at all. He just wanted. He still wants. His stomach is tight with want and his erection is painful with need. It won't go away. It's all-encompassing, that need, and he had to run, so it's still there. He has to ignore it. It will go away eventually. He hopes.

He slams the car door and is halfway up the path to the house when he remembers the knife. He walks back down to the car, grabs it from the passenger's seat, and, with it in his hand, heads back up the path toward the house.

Once inside, he pushes the front door closed quietly, not wanting to wake his wife or the kids, and locks the dead-bolt and the chain.

Then he walks to the kitchen and turns on the light above the sink. He sets the knife in the metal basin and turns on the hot water. He squirts dish soap onto his hands and scrubs them. They're rough and callused and hangnails are peeling themselves away, revealing the meat beneath. He feels like the blood will never wash off – but he felt that way last time this happened, too.

He rinses his hands under the steaming tap. The water is almost painfully hot. It makes his hands tingle. He watches the pink water run down the drain in a counter-clockwise swirl.

He picks up the large kitchen knife and scrubs the

blood off with a green sponge and once it's washed and rinsed he puts it in the dish drainer where he found it earlier this evening.

His erection has not gone down and it aches but he tries to ignore it.

Think about something else, he tells himself, which only makes him think of the attack earlier this evening, the interrupted attack. He almost had her. She was almost his.

He shakes his head, trying to dislodge the thought.

He shuts off the light above the sink and walks out of the kitchen.

William pushes a door open and looks inside. He can see his two daughters lying together in their bed, hugging each other. He knows it's only from the street lamp's light coming in through the window – coming in between the dusty slatted blinds – but they appear to be glowing. They look like angels to him, beautiful shining angels. He can't imagine how someone as vile as himself could be even partially responsible for creating them. How could they possibly have come from him, all shining and beautiful and new?

The eight-year-old lifts her head up and looks at him.

'What are you doing, daddy?'

'Go back to sleep, honey,' he says, pulling the door closed.

*

In the bathroom, William puts down the toilet lid and sits on the toilet. Using the brush his wife usually uses to scrub the bathtub, he goes at his boots. He scrubs at them for a few minutes, rinses the brush under the hot water running from the tub's faucet, and then scrubs some more. But he's not thinking about what he's doing. All he can think about is that girl. He doesn't know what's wrong with him. He wasn't raised to be like this. And that poor girl. It could have been anyone. If another woman had walked by five minutes earlier it would have been her instead. Or if he'd found a different place hidden in shadows. Or if that man who'd bummed a smoke off him had asked him why he was just standing around out there. That poor girl. He feels sad about it, and yet he wants nothing so much as to go back and finish what he started. He wants nothing so much as that. He aches for it.

He rinses the brush under the hot water one last time, then turns off the bathtub faucet.

Someone should have stopped him.

Goddamn it, he wishes this erection would go away.

He unties his boots and pulls his sweaty feet out of them. Then he stands and steps out of his jeans. They got blood on them, too, but it's not much. After a couple of washes it won't even be recognizable as blood.

He takes off his sweater and his undershirt and walks out of the bathroom wearing only his dirty-water colored underwear.

*

As William falls into bed, Elaine rolls over to face him, flipping her pillow as she does. He can see her eyes looking at him and he wonders if she can hear his heart pounding in his chest. She must be able to; it's like a drum.

She smells good, like shampoo and cocoa butter and sweat.

'Where you been?'

'Went for a walk.'

'I heard the car.'

William doesn't want to talk. He reaches out and strokes Elaine's breast, but she pushes his hand away. He leans forward and tries to kiss her, but she turns her head away, too, and he ends up kissing her neck.

'Not now,' she says.

He reaches out to stroke her other breast, thumbing her nipple. She pushes him away again, this time with more force.

'Not. Now.'

William rolls onto his back, looks at the ceiling. There's something wrong with his guts. There's something in his guts that won't let him stop. There's a need there, deep in there, and it just won't let him stop. It's hungry and it's got control of him and it won't let him stop. He has to go back. It's Elaine's fault. He has to go back and finish what he started. Even if it means the police get him, even if it means he goes to jail for the rest of his life – that might even be a good thing: he'd no longer have to hide what he is from his wife and children, he'd no longer be able to hurt anyone else. But he has to finish this one last thing. He has to go back.

He sits up in bed and spins, swinging his feet off the edge.

'What are you doing?'

'Going out.'

'Where? You just got in.'

'Just out,' he says, and stands.

He gets dressed in the bathroom, slipping back into his pants and shoes and sweater.

He grabs the kitchen knife from the dish drainer and walks back out into the night.

22

Frank makes a left and drives down a one-way street. As he drives, the row houses give way to Tudor-style single-family homes. He looks left and right as he goes, looks for a stroller that's been knocked to its side. He drives for three blocks, seeing nothing.

Then, as he swerves the Skylark slightly to the left to avoid a pothole, one of his headlights catches it lying on its side between two parked cars. He can only see the blue canvas back of it and the chrome handles and the wheels with black treads. What's inside of the stroller is facing the opposite direction.

'Oh, shit.'

He simply sits with a foot on the brake pedal, his hands gripping the steering wheel, and one headlight shining on a mangled stroller. He lets go of the steering wheel with both hands and then wraps his fingers around it again. It feels grimy under his palms, grimy and hot.

He closes his eyes and opens them again.

All right, he thinks.

He puts the car in reverse and backs into the curb, hitting it once, straightening out, parking, and then killing the engine.

He steps from the car and the cold air hits him. The inside of the car was about ten degrees hotter and he'd not had the heater on. He was simply nervous and sweating and filling the car with his own body heat. As the cold air hits him, it sends a shiver up his spine, chilling the sweat that stands out on his body. He stands unmoving by his car for a moment and in that moment he considers simply getting back in and driving away, driving away and never looking back. But he doesn't do that; he couldn't do that, despite the fleeting thought. He could never live with himself. He could never look at himself in the mirror and see the man he believes himself to be; he'd only see a coward.

He remembers something that his dad told him before he died. All courageous men are afraid, he told Frank – all of them: if a man isn't afraid of something that normal men are afraid of, that doesn't make him courageous, it makes him an idiot. A courageous man is a man who feels fear but does what he has to do anyway. If you're not afraid, he told Frank, you're not being brave.

'You're right, dad,' Frank whispers into the night.

He nods. He nods and he takes his first step toward the stroller. It is followed by a second step, and then a third.

He stops walking once he has reached the back of the

stroller. Then he puts out his foot and turns the stroller toward him with his black leather shoe, cringing in anticipation as he does, but when he sees an arm he stops.

'Oh, God,' he says.

He leans down and turns the stroller toward him with his hands, revealing what's on the other side. A pink leg. A baby's lolling head.

No.

He blinks.

His heart is pounding so hard he can feel it behind his ears, throbbing there, and in his temples. He realizes he's been holding his breath and lets himself exhale. He swallows.

And then he sees it for what it really is. A doll – a child's doll strapped into a stroller. Flesh-colored, one glass-blue eye staring at Frank. Where the other eye should be is just a black cavity. Maybe some boy pried it out with the prongs of a fork to add to his marble collection; maybe the doll was dropped and the eye popped out, rolling to some unreachable location. Either way – gone.

A shocked laugh croaks from Frank's throat and surprises him so much that he actually glances around to see where it could have come from.

When he realizes it was him, he laughs again.

A fucking doll.

Stroller probably spent five years in a hall closet before some little girl found it there, strapped her doll in it, and rolled it around the neighborhood till the sun started to dip below the evening horizon and her mom called her in to eat her chicken livers, peas and mashed potatoes, leaving it in the street for Erin to hit in the dark hours of the next morning while she drove home from her long night shift, half asleep, thinking about something that happened at work.

Frank gets to his feet, feels a brief rush of dizziness that quickly passes, turns, and walks toward his car.

'Oh, thank God,' Erin says into the the telephone. 'Come home. I want you to hold me.'

She feels her legs go weak and she falls into a chair.

She wants him home, looking into her eyes, smiling at her; she wants to feel his big arms wrapped around her, making her safe.

'I'm on my way,' Frank says. 'I'll be there soon.'

'Thank you,' she says. 'I love you.' Erin feels as if someone has lifted a boulder off her chest. 'I love you so much.'

'I love you too,' he says, and puts the scratched-up pay phone back in its cradle. He stands a moment smiling at the absurdity of this, at the fact that it was all over a one-eyed doll, and then he turns away from the phone and heads toward his car, which is parked across the street.

He reaches the curb, and when he sees no headlights coming at him from either direction, he jogs across. As he crosses the street, he sees that a police cruiser is parked two cars behind his own. He sees that a police officer is sitting behind the wheel. He sees that the police officer is watching him.

Frank tilts his head in the cop's direction, howdy, and continues to his car, but the cop does not reciprocate. He just stares.

Frank gets into his car, and he sits down, pulling the door closed.

He glances in the rearview mirror; the cop is watching him.

Frank starts his car; a moment later he hears the cop's car start.

He puts his left turn signal on and pulls his Skylark out into the quiet street and he heads toward home; the round yellow headlights of the cop car pull out after him.

23

Peter Adams paces back and forth, wearing out the rug beneath his feet. Ron and Bettie simply sit on the couch beside one another. They're holding hands and watching him silently.

But he just paces – paces.

This isn't right. This shouldn't have happened. He doesn't understand how this happened. It doesn't make sense. It doesn't. He's a good person – he tries to be. How can a good person be in this situation? It's stupid. It's fucking stupid and it doesn't make sense.

'You should go talk to her,' Ron says.

Peter stops pacing a moment and looks at Ron.

Ron simply looks back, no readable expression on his face – as if he wasn't the one who got Peter into this mess, as if the whole swapping thing wasn't his idea in the first place.

'I don't want to talk to her,' he says finally.

'You're making a mistake,' Ron says.

'Fuck you.'

'I'm trying to help you.'

'I don't want to fucking talk to you,' Peter says, and turns to Bettie. 'How can you say that all we shared was sex?' He hears a childish whine in his own voice that he hates.

'Because,' Ron says, 'all you shared was sex. That was the whole point.'

'I don't want to fucking talk to you,' Peter says again; and then says, 'You think you're above it all, don't you? You think you're so fucking enlightened. Well, I wasn't talking to you. I was talking to Bettie.'

'No, you weren't talking to me,' Ron says, calmly, making Peter hate him more: Peter wishes the guy would get mad, would be unreasonable – this is an unreasonable situation and calls for unreasonable behavior, goddamn it, not simple calm – 'but you were talking to my wife, and in situations like this, I feel pretty comfortable speaking for her. Especially when I'm only echoing what she's already said for herself.'

'Situations like this?'

'Bettie is my wife. Just because you two had sex does not mean you earned a right to her love. You didn't. That's reserved for me. The sooner you get that through your skull, the sooner you can mend things with your own wife, and the better off you'll be.'

'Go fuck yourself,' Peter says, turning away from Ron.

But only a moment later, he turns back around. 'Would you please just let me talk to Bettie alone? Please.' Again that childish whine in his voice. He hates himself for it but he can't stop it. A grown man whining. A grown man with manicured fingernails and perfect hair whining. A grown man who knows more about good merlot than he'll ever know about internal combustion engines – whining. He can't believe how much he hates himself right now. 'Please,' he says again.

'She's already said she's not interested in what you have to offer.'

'Because you're fucking sitting here! Let me talk to her alone.'

'Ron,' Bettie says.

He looks at her.

'It's okay.'

'You sure?'

She nods.

'Okay,' Ron says, getting to his feet. 'Fine.'

24

The clock on the nightstand says it's four fifty, but neither Thomas nor Christopher is looking at it. Christopher is belly-down on the mattress, and Thomas is on top of him, covered in a gloss of sweat, holding himself up with a hand pressed down on Christopher's back between his shoulder blades. Both men are silent during the last of it save for quick short breaths from Thomas and then it is over.

Thomas rolls off Christopher, the guilt hitting him before he's even on his back, and he stares up at the ceiling.

Christopher gets to his feet.

'I'm gonna clean up,' he says. 'I'll be right back.'

Thomas nods but he does not make eye contact. He can't, not after what they've done.

He simply stares at the ceiling.

There is a yellow water stain there shaped sort of like a crescent moon drawn by a child and Thomas tries to figure out how it got there. There shouldn't be any plumbing there. Directly overhead should just be another bedroom. Maybe it's a child's room and the child is a bed wetter. Maybe his upstairs neighbors have a plant there that they perpetually overwater. He doesn't know. He doesn't really care. It's just another stain in a world full of stains.

Thomas reaches to the nightstand for his cigarettes, puts one between his lips, strikes a match. He's always liked the smell of matches. When he was small, around ten or eleven, and found boxes of them, he would burn them one after the other just so he could smell the sulfur exploding with the flame, and since his grandmother was a two-pack-a-day smoker and forgetful to boot, he found boxes of them everywhere, littered throughout the house.

He also found bottles of gin and vermouth hidden away, which he tasted and cringed over and then put back. At the time he didn't know it was impossible for grandma to have obtained the liquor legally but he did know she sneaked her drinks, pouring herself a mixture from the two bottles into juice cups when she thought he wasn't around, adding olives, and sipping them while smoking and listening to her shows. He'd heard of Prohibition, of course – heard the word, anyway – but he didn't connect it with grandma's juice-cup drinks until much later; nor did he connect her often leaving him alone in the house and coming home smelling of fermentation only a year or two later with Roosevelt or the Cullen-Harrison Act or the sudden visibility of drinking establishments.

He did however connect her forgetfulness with her

drinking; if he asked for his allowance after she'd had three or four, he found he could usually ask for it again the very next day and often would get it.

He inhales deeply on his cigarette, feeling depressed, lost.

This shouldn't have happened.

He pushes himself off the bed and looks around for his pants, having no idea where he left them. Finally he sees a wrinkled fabric leg sticking out from under the bed. He pulls the pants out of the shadows as if they were an animal trying to escape, shakes off the dust bunnies they collected from the floor, from under the bed, and slips back into them.

Then sits back down on the edge of the mattress and continues to smoke.

After the first cigarette has been smoked down to the filter, he lights a new one with it, and butts it out in the glass ashtray sitting on the nightstand.

Soon enough, too soon, Christopher walks out of the bathroom wearing a pair of underpants and nothing else. Thomas wishes he would get dressed. He should at least put some pants on. Thomas doesn't want to see his body; it only reminds him of what happened here tonight.

Thomas glances at his face, but briefly, and then looks away.

'Maybe you should leave,' he says.

Christopher stops in his tracks and looks at Thomas.

Thomas can feel Christopher looking at him but he refuses to look back.

'What?' Christopher says.

'Maybe you should leave.'

Christopher continues to stand there motionless for a long time. He doesn't say anything and he doesn't move. He certainly doesn't leave.

Then finally he says, 'May I have a cigarette?'

Thomas nods but doesn't make any motion to give him one.

Christopher walks to the nightstand, retrieves a cigarette from the pack himself, and lights it with a match. The smell of sulfur fills the air. Then he just stands there, watching the match burn in his fingers, and once the flame reaches his fingertips, he grabs the head of the match, which is no longer aflame but seems like it must still be hot, and lets the flame burn the rest of the small stick. Once the entire match is burned, the fuel spent, the flame goes out on its own and Christopher drops it into the ashtray amongst a litter of ash and butts and fingernail clippings.

Thomas notices that there is a lot of dust on the baseboards. A lot of dust.

He wonders who first called them baseboards.

'I've never done that before,' he says.

Christopher takes a drag from his cigarette and sits down beside him.

'Are you upset with me?'

Thomas shakes his head.

'I'm disgusted with myself for this,' he says. 'This was a mistake and I'm disgusted with myself.'

'Why?'

'Why what?'

'Why was it a mistake?'

Thomas shrugs.

'I don't know. It was wrong.'

Then he glances over at Christopher, making his first attempt at eye contact since Christopher re-entered the bedroom; it's a fleeting thing, and he almost immediately looks away, back to the baseboards. It's strange that he's never noticed how much dust they collect.

'I've spent my entire life,' he says, 'trying to be normal. Telling myself . . . I don't know . . . telling myself that I've simply never found the right woman. Telling myself . . .' He shakes his head. 'I'm gonna have to quit the bowling team.'

He shouldn't even be alive right now. If he'd killed himself when he'd planned to this never would have happened. He should have pulled the trigger as soon as he heard the knock on the door. He should have just pulled the fucking trigger. Christopher might have kicked the door in and found him but this never would happened and that'd be something at least. It would be better than this, better than what he's feeling right now.

'We didn't do anything wrong,' Christopher says.

Thomas takes a drag from his cigarette, then waves it

over the ashtray, flicking his thumb against the filter as he does, dropping the spent bit into it. His lungs feel hot. He looks at the pile of ashes and butts and fingernail clippings in the tray.

Someone should invent a baseboard duster, something on a long stick so people wouldn't have to bend down. Maybe someone already has. He'll have to look into it.

'Thomas,' Christopher says.

'What?'

'We didn't do anything wrong.'

Thomas scrapes a bit of dead skin off his lower lip with his teeth, gets it on the end of his tongue, and spits, as if it were a seed husk. He doesn't see where it goes.

'Would you tell anyone what we did?' he says.

Christopher doesn't respond for a moment. Then: 'No.'

'Why not?'

'It would end friendships,' Christopher says. 'It would . . .' and he trails off.

Thomas nods.

'It's shameful,' he says. 'How can something be shameful but not be wrong?' And then answers his own question. 'It can't,' he says.

He takes another drag at his cigarette and looks at the wall.

'It's shameful,' Christopher says, 'because we're told to be ashamed of it.'

'Maybe.'

'How can something that hurts nobody be wrong?'

'I don't feel good about it,' Thomas says. 'I feel like I made a mistake. I feel like I've done something wrong.'

'Because you've been told it's wrong all your life,' Christopher says. 'So you feel bad about it, and since you feel bad, you think it must be wrong. But we didn't steal anything. We didn't hurt anyone. We simply . . .' He coughs into his hand and looks away. 'You know,' he says, 'right now we're sending kids to Vietnam to kill people over ideas. We're sending boys right out of high school over there to kill people who never threatened any violence against us simply because we've decided they think the wrong things.' He laughs. 'And yet it's what you and I did here tonight that's supposed to be shameful.'

'I don't know if it's as simple as that.'

'Maybe not,' Christopher says, 'but you get my point.'

'I get your point.'

'Good.'

Then Christopher reaches his hand out toward Thomas. He doesn't touch him, but he reaches out his hand and lets it settle on the mattress near him.

'I like you, Thomas,' he says.

'I like you too,' Thomas says.

Then he looks up and makes eye contact again, but this time he holds it. He nods his head, as much to himself, he thinks, as to Christopher.

'I do,' he says.

25

The clock strikes five. The cow goes moo.

26

David is in the back with Mr. Vacanti while John drives the ambulance toward the hospital. Unconscious, Mr. Vacanti is strapped down on the stretcher, tied down tight – for his own safety, of course.

'Slow down,' David yells over the sound of sirens.

'He's got internal bleeding,' John says. 'He'll die.'

'Then he'll die. I've got business with him.'

'Take care of it, then, because I ain't slowing down.'

David breaks a capsule of smelling salts under Mr. Vacanti's nose and watches the brown paper surrounding the capsule turn dark, and the man inhales, gasps, coughs, opens eyes which momentarily roll around in his head like overgreased ball bearings. Veins are broken in his left eye, and it's pooling with blood.

His eyes eventually find focus, and he looks up at David; and when he does confusion passes over his face like the shadow of a cloud.

'Davey?' he says with hesitation. 'Davey White?'

'Except it's David now.'

'What are you doing here?'

'Wrong question, Mr. Vacanti.'

'What?'

David reaches out with two fingers and taps the shelf of glass jutting from Mr. Vacanti's forehead as if it were a table top and he were making a point that needed emphasizing. The man yelps in pain. He tries to bat David's hand away but he can't move. David watches panic light in his eyes as he realizes he is strapped down. Strapped down tight. He looks down at his unmoving wrists and then back up at David.

'What's going on?' he says. 'What are you doing here?'

'I already told you that's the wrong question, Mr. Vacanti,' David says, and as he hits the last hard syllable he taps the glass shelf jutting from Mr. Vacanti's head again. Another yelp. 'The correct question is, what are *you* doing here. And the answer is, you were in a car accident. An ambulance was called. And I happen to be a paramedic. Unfortunately, your injuries,' and he grabs the shelf jutting from Mr. Vacanti's forehead and gives it a little shake, 'are beyond my scope. And the hospital. Well,' he laughs, 'let's just say I don't think you're gonna make it.'

David reaches into his hip pocket and retrieves a flask. He unscrews the top and takes a nip. It burns his throat and it feels good. He follows the first hit with a second. The liquid warms his insides. His chest feels as if it's got a small fire burning inside it.

'What's wrong with me?' Mr. Vacanti asks.

'That's a question you should have asked yourself decades ago.'

David takes one last swallow from his flask before twisting the cap back on and tucking it away. Twenty-six years he went without seeing this son of a bitch and he turns up like this. Twenty-six years. He'd almost been able to make himself forget. He'd only thought of him once or twice a year this last decade. He'd almost been able to forget.

'Preventative medicine is the thing,' he says. 'I mean, if you had asked yourself what was wrong with you way back when, if you had been able to stop your sickness, well . . . my guess is you wouldn't be dying today, Mr. Vacanti.'

Mr. Vacanti tries to pull himself out of the straps holding him down. He struggles, pulling hard, turning his hands purple, gritting his teeth, grunting, his whole body going taut, but finally – of course – giving up.

'You won't be able to forgive yourself for this,' he tells David.

David nods.

'That's probably true,' he says. 'After all, I haven't been able to forgive you. I guess I'm just not the forgiving sort, am I, Mr. Vacanti? But then, I'm not a predator of children, either. We've all got our flaws, right?'

He waits for a response but Mr. Vacanti only stares. It's

well enough; there's nothing the son of a bitch could say anyway.

'But here's the thing,' David says. 'Even if I can't forgive myself, I'll be able to live with myself. I'm sure of that. I'll be able to live with myself. What I can't live with is letting you get away with what you did, not when this opportunity has been handed to me.'

He nods to himself.

'I didn't want to . . .' Mr. Vacanti says, trailing off.

'But you *did*,' David snaps at him. Then he smiles and pinches Mr. Vacanti's bloody cheek. 'Just do what I say and it'll all be over soon enough,' he says. 'Maybe it won't even hurt.' He scratches his chin where beard is growing in. 'Do you remember that, Mr. Vacanti?'

After a moment's pause, Mr. Vacanti shakes his head.

'That's a direct quote,' David says. 'Any guess as to who I'm quoting?'

There is a moment of silence.

'Me,' Mr. Vacanti says finally, not looking at him.

'Bingo,' David says, and taps at the shard of glass jutting from Mr. Vacanti's head for emphasis. 'Bing. Go. Got it in one guess. God, you're sharp. No pun intended—' looking at the shard of glass. 'It's no wonder you're a teacher. Kids just have so much they need to learn, don't they? And you're just the one to teach them.'

They must be getting near the hospital. That can't happen. They can't get there, not with Mr. Vacanti still breathing.

'Wait here,' David says to the strapped-down Mr. Vacanti before heading to the front of the vehicle where John is busy driving.

'Listen to me,' David says. 'I want you to pull over.'

'He's gonna bleed to death,' John says. 'I'm taking him in.'

'You don't understand this,' David says.

'I understand enough to know that I'm not stopping.'

'I'm asking you as a friend,' David says. 'We can slice one of the tires. We'll say we got a flat. No one will ever fucking know. You don't have to do anything but stop the ambulance. I'll take care of the rest.' He wipes at the corners of his mouth. 'No one will know,' he says again.

'I'll know,' John says. 'I'll know that we killed a man whose life we were supposed to save. I don't know what your history with him is but it's turning you blood-simple and I'm not gonna be a part of it.'

'Goddamn it, John,' David says. 'We're friends. I'm asking you, please.'

'We are friends. And in the five years we've worked together, I've never seen this kind of shit from you before, so I'm willing to bet whatever he did to you was serious, and I'm really fucking sorry for that, David. I am. But I won't be party to killing him. I just won't.'

'Don't you understand? I don't want to kill him. I just don't want to save him.'

'It's our job,' John says. 'People do jobs they don't want to do all the fucking time.'

'Not like this, they don't.'

'You can't kill him.'

'I already told you, I don't want to kill him.'

'Not saving him when you can save him is the same goddamn thing and you know it. Only it's a coward's murder.
Now you listen to me, David. I'm driving this ambulance
the rest of the way to the hospital without any fucking stops.
If you got a problem with that man back there, it's yours to
deal with.'

David wants to make him understand, wants to say
something so he'll understand, but he knows that nothing
he can say will change John's mind.

David turns away from him and starts toward the back
of the ambulance.

'David,' John says.

David looks at him.

'I'm sorry.'

'Yeah, I know,' David says, and makes his way to the
back.

27

Unable to walk, Kat crawls toward her apartment. She can't be more than ten feet away, but even that short distance seems insuperable. She feels cold and weak. She has bled so much. It's splattered across the courtyard. She can barely move – but she does move. One hand in front of the other, one skinned knee in front of the other.

Easy-peasy, she tells herself. Just move your arm six inches, press it against the concrete and pull yourself forward. Like pouring a drink. Like changing a tire. It's a simple task – simple.

She crawls through the darkness of early morning and she tries not to pass out and she keeps telling that part of her that wants to let go, that wants to quit, to shut up, just shut up.

It's so loud now, that part of her.

Just let the darkness come, it says. It'll be easier. It'll be easier, and maybe afterwards, when you wake, you'll find this was all just a bad dream.

But she knows if she lets go, if she quits, if she lets the darkness come, she won't wake. She'll never open her eyes again. She wishes that wasn't the truth, but it is, and she knows it.

She can still feel people watching her. She can't see them now – her head is down and she doesn't have the energy to look at anything but the tiny pebbles imbedded in the concrete she's crawling upon, tiny smooth pebbles that look as if they've been polished in a riverbed – but she can feel them, those eyes, those people watching her. They don't make a sound. But they're there, and they do not help.

She pulls herself forward another six inches. She's not going to die out here. She's not going to allow herself to die out here.

Putting one arm in front of the other, sliding her body across the cold concrete being made warm by her heat, as her body is made cold by the night, pulling herself forward on her now raw arms, Kat manages to move herself five feet nearer her apartment. It is such an exhausting, painful, Sisyphean task that, though she halves her distance to the front door, getting that last five feet seems harder than getting ten feet did when she began.

She is so tired. She is so cold. She hurts so bad.

But she can see the keys now. She can see them hanging

from the doorknob. From the doorknob in the closed door
– closed.

How will she be able to reach the doorknob?

Three and a half feet off the ground, it might as well be
ten feet off the ground – or twenty.

Why did the wind have to blow the door shut?

Why does God hate her?

What did she do?

What did she do to deserve this?

God damn Him.

God damn Him, why does He hate her?

Stop. Stop, she tells herself. You can't let yourself fall
apart again: it costs too much: it spends too much energy.
You need all the energy you have left. You need all the
energy you've got left, so just stop, stop now. You can fall
apart later. Once you're safe. You can slip into the warm
water of a warm bath and you can fall apart then. But not
now. Right now you've got to get to that door. You can do
that much. Don't worry about turning the doorknob yet;
don't worry about pushing the door open yet. Just get to
the door, Kat. You can do that. You're strong and you can
do that.

Easy-peasy, she tells herself.

Easy-peasy.

Like pouring a drink, she tells herself. Like changing
a tire.

She focuses on the keys. She won't take her eyes off them.
She focuses on the keys and she puts one raw, raggedly

skinless arm forward, and she pulls herself bodily six inches closer to the door. Six inches closer, she thinks. Four and a half feet. I only have to do that nine more times, she thinks, and I'll be there. And she does it again. Eight more, she thinks.

Eight.

Attainable goals, she thinks.

Like pouring a drink.

Then she hears a noise from the street that makes her panic.

She hears the sound of a vehicle pulling to the curb and coming to a stop. She wants to believe it's help. She wants to believe it's someone who will see her and say oh my God, you poor thing, you poor, poor thing, what's happened to you, let me help, but it's not.

She recognizes the loose, jangly rattle of the engine. She's heard it before. She heard it immediately after the man who attacked her ran away, ran out to the street. It's his car, and he's come back. He must have come back.

She can see the light of the headlights splashing across the oak trees at the front of the building.

Don't panic, she thinks.

And then she puts an arm forward and pulls her body forward behind it.

Seven, she thinks.

The headlights go out.

She puts her other arm forward.

The engine goes quiet.

Six, she thinks.

A squeaking car door opens and she hears feet hit asphalt.

Five, she thinks.

Don't panic.

The door slams shut and she hears footsteps coming nearer.

Four, she thinks. Don't panic.

Four, she thinks.

28

Frank watches in his sideview mirror as a pair of legs scissor their way around the police cruiser's door, as they head toward him. The police cruiser followed him for only a few hundred yards before its light flashed and the cop waved him to the curb. And then sat. They sat on the side of the road for several minutes before the cop finally pushed open the driver's side door of his patrol car and stepped from within, Frank getting more nervous as each second passed. But now the cop is walking toward him, holding a bright flashlight up by his right shoulder as he walks.

Frank sits stiff, his hands on the steering wheel. The guy's trouble, obvious trouble, and Frank doesn't want him to claim that he was reaching for something, that he thought Frank had a gun, say, and that's why Frank is dead. He knows it doesn't really make sense, doesn't really matter – if the cop wants to shoot him or do something else he's just gonna do it and he can make up whatever he wants – but Frank will take no chances.

A chest fills Frank's driver's side window. A flashlight beam shines in bright so that when Frank tries to look at the cop standing outside his car he can't see anything but an explosion of blinding light. It's like trying to see someone clearly when they're backlit by the sun.

'Good morning,' the cop says.

'Morning, officer. Something the matter?'

'You don't know why I stopped you?'

'Should I know, sir?'

'You being smart with me?'

'No, sir. I just don't know why you pulled me over.'

'Then that's what you shoulda said in the first place. I'm the one asking the questions.'

'Okay, sir.'

'Give me your keys.'

'That's not a question, sir. I don't mean you any disrespect, but I just don't know why you would need my keys.'

'And you don't need to know.'

'Sir?'

'Someone fitting your description was seen fleeing the site of a burglary,' the cop says. 'I'm gonna check your trunk.'

'Fitting my description?'

'You're colored, aren't you?'

'Yes, sir.'

'Then he fit your description.'

Frank doesn't move.

'If there's nothing in your trunk, you got nothing to worry about. I'll give you back your keys and you can be on your merry way to wherever colored folks go at five o'clock in the morning.' The cop puts the beam of light directly into Frank's eyes. 'Is there something in your trunk?'

'No, sir.'

But he still doesn't move.

'Give me your fuckin' keys before I lose my temper.'

Frank reaches to the ignition and slowly pulls out his key and hands a ring of them over to the cop. The cop takes them, snapping them violently out of Frank's hand.

'Don't move,' the cop says. 'Just sit here and be a good boy.'

The cop smiles, taps the roof of Frank's car, and then turns and walks away. Frank can see him walk to the back of his Skylark and pop the trunk. Then the trunk lid swings up, blocking Frank's view of the cop and his car.

He does not like this. Something is wrong. He checks his glove box for an old pack of Chesterfields but finds nothing. Frank quit smoking two years ago – mostly. Now he only smokes in moments like this. There have been a lot of moments like this tonight.

He hears a noise that sounds like it might have come from the cop car, a door opening or something, a squeak. He hears a grunt. He wants to get out of his car and see what's going on but he doesn't want to get shot. He feels trapped in here.

When he was in the army he often had to deal with officers that acted just like this cop. Lieutenants, second lieutenants, fresh out of academy and simply handed their rank. They were green and still high on their new found authority. They were the most likely to give you shit about having your sideburns a bit too long. About not having shaved close enough. About not saluting immediately or sharply enough. About not having your BDU in perfect condition, crisp and ready for war. Your boots gotta shine if you're gonna bayonet a son of a bitch, private. I wanna see my reflection in 'em. They thought they owned the fucking world because they were simply handed authority without having to earn it, without having to earn it or the respect that should come with it. They thought respect came with the lieutenant insignia they bought down at the PX. Soldiers hated them – the privates and specialists Frank knew, anyway – and this cop is just like that. Some people get a uniform and they think they answer to no one. Or they know they answer to someone and they hate it, but the rest of the world better watch out, goddamn it, because the rest of the world answers to *them*.

Frank hears a thud, and his car groans, his rear shocks squeak.

What's going on back there?

Why is he taking so long to find nothing?

Frank closes his eyes.

If he gets through this he may take up smoking full-time again.

He hears the sound of something metal – he thinks – dropping to the asphalt, and then a whispered, 'Shit,' and then a scraping sound, maybe the sound of it – the metal thing that dropped – being picked up.

He looks in the driver's side mirror but sees nothing on the street-side but empty. He looks in the passenger's side mirror next, but too late; all he sees is a blue blur of cop disappearing behind his car, hidden by his open trunk's lid.

He hears a clatter and then silence.

'Sir,' the cop says after a while. 'Sir, would you please step from your vehicle.'

Truth is, he'd rather not, but he pushes the door open and swings his body around, stepping out of the car, closing the door behind him. He cannot see the cop. The cop is hidden by the trunk lid, but he thinks the cop is watching him – no, he knows the cop is watching him.

He doesn't like this at all.

He exhales and inhales and walks toward the trunk of the car.

Something bad is about to happen and just because he doesn't know what doesn't mean he doesn't know it won't be pretty. It won't be pretty for him, anyway. He tries to brace himself for whatever it is, but that's a hard thing to do, brace yourself, when you don't know what direction you're about to fall in.

He walks around the back of his car, around the raised trunk lid, and as soon as he does, the cop grabs Frank by the back of his neck with a rubber-gloved hand – rubber gloves? – and shoves him toward the trunk, shining his flashlight inside it as he does.

'What the fuck is this?' the cop says, spittle flying from his mouth.

'I don't—' he begins, but then stops. Because he does. He does know. He knows exactly. And he knows, too, there's nothing he can say or do to avoid this turning ugly fast.

'That's the television you just put in my trunk, sir,' he says.

The cop slams the flashlight into Frank's gut, bending him over. He feels the air rush out of his body and he hears himself groaning.

'Fuck,' he says, gasping for air.

'Smart-mouth nigger,' the cops says. 'A man was killed in his own home not half a mile from here. Killed with a tire iron. Bludgeoned to death. That tire iron looks like it's got blood on it to me. Is it yours?'

'How do you know it was a tire iron he was bludgeoned with?'

Another swing to the gut.

'Answer the question. Is it yours?'

'If it's got blood on it, it's not.' Gasping.

'That's pretty fucking convenient.'

'It's the truth.'

'It's in your trunk.'

'It's not mine.'

'Pick it up and take a closer look, and then tell me it isn't yours.'

Frank is just getting his breath back. He stands up and straightens out, breathing in and breathing out. He looks at the cop. He swallows.

'Pick it up and take a closer look,' the cop says again.

'I will not,' Frank says. 'I'm not touching it, sir.'

'Pick up the fucking tire iron,' the cop says, more spittle flying from his mouth, some of it splashing on Frank's neck. Frank does not move to wipe it off.

'No, sir.'

'You think you're smart? Pick up the tire iron or I'll fucking kill you.'

'If you kill me, I'll be dead and you'll have no one to frame for whatever it is you're trying to frame me for, sir,' Frank says. 'Murder, it sounds like.'

'You think you're smarter than me?'

'No, sir.'

'You ain't smarter than me. I got no problem framing a dead man. Fact is, though, I don't even need you dead. I don't need you dead and I don't want you dead. I want to teach you something about mouthing off to your betters, though,' he says, nodding. 'I do want that. Smart-mouth nigger. When you wake up, you're gonna learn something.'

And with that, the cop swings the flashlight at Frank's head, cracking it across his skull. The flashlight breaks, the plastic shattering, flying off in several directions. The batteries fall out and scatter like cockroaches when the kitchen light's turned on.

But Frank does not fall.

He is dazed though and is trying to blink the dazed feeling away, trying to blink his vision back into existence, when the cop pulls out his billy club and slams it across his forehead.

This time Frank does fall.

He can feel himself going down, dropping to his knees.

The ground rushes up at him.

He sees a penny, face up, near the back-right tire of his car.

Good luck penny, he thinks.

And then he falls flat on his face and he doesn't think anything else – not for a while, anyway.

29

Alan looks at the poor stupid motherfucker lying on the ground in front of him. The guy's face-down on the asphalt, blood leaking from a split in the swelling lump on his forehead.

He's already working out his story for having to club the guy. He doesn't need much. He caught the son of a bitch red-handed, the guy resisted arrest, and Alan had to restrain him with force. A lot of force. That's all. That'll be plenty. It has been in the past. Who trusts a civilian over a cop? No one. Even civilians don't trust civilians over cops; put the testimony of a cop against the testimony of a guy who claims he didn't do it, your honor, I swear, and you get a conviction every time – every fucking time. Especially if the guy's colored.

Alan slides the billy club back into his belt, bends down, and flips the guy over. Heavy son of a bitch. Alan is lucky he didn't fight back. He suspects he might have lost that match. Once the guy's on his back, Alan has to heft the TV back out of the trunk. He's goddamn tired of hauling it around and he's glad it's almost over with. Whoever invented the television should have made it lighter. Jesus. He sets it on the guy's chest, holding it balanced there with one hand. With his other hand, he grabs the guy's right arm and presses his fingerprints onto the surface of the television. One set of fingerprints done, he drops one arm, picks up the other, and presses some prints into the other side. Best to be thorough.

With the fingerprints planted on it, Alan puts the TV back into the trunk.

Then he takes out the tire iron. As he's pulling it out of the trunk, he decides he'll have to hit himself with it. Once on the arm and once on the neck. Just for safe measure.

Then he'll drop it by the unconscious colored bastard and call for backup. The guy went for the tire iron, see, hit me, I had to fight him, and I took him down. He almost got away, but I took him down.

Alan nods. That's how it'll go, he decides.

He may even get an MPD medal for this.

He grabs the cold metal in his gloved right hand, standing there in the morning darkness by the side of the road. He looks at the sticky blood drying on its surface. He breathes in and out.

'Okay.'

He swings his fist and the tire iron in it toward his neck, but misses the soft part he was aiming for. The tire iron slams into his jaw and his ear instead – with an audible metal-on-bone *crack!* – and pain shoots out in every direction from the contact point in a jagged ripple.

He drops the tire iron.

'God fucking *damn* it,' he shouts through gritted teeth as blood begins to leak from his ear. He stomps the asphalt. 'Fuck!' He stomps around in an angry, pained circle, then manages to regain his senses. He touches his ear, looks at the blood on his fingertips. He hears nothing but a high-pitched hum in that ear, as if it had an insect trapped inside it.

'It better be temporary, you fuck,' Alan says, kicking Frank in the ribs. Frank groans but doesn't come to.

Then Alan picks up the tire iron again and holds out his left arm.

'Okay,' he says. 'Try not to break it.'

He licks his lips, looks at the spot on his arm where he plans to hit himself, swallows.

Blood drips from his earlobe and splashes warm on his shoulder.

'Okay,' he says again.

Then he swings.

30

Kat is barely standing. She is leaning against the cold stone wall in front of her apartment – hidden in the shadows of her front porch – or she wouldn't be standing at all; without the wall to lean on, she couldn't stand. But she is standing. She's here, only inches from her front door, standing in the shadows. She has no idea how she managed to get here, but here she is.

The man who attacked her stands only fifteen or so feet away. The kitchen knife is in his hand. He stands half in the shadows and half in the light of the courtyard. He turns in a circle, looking for her.

'I know you're out here somewhere,' he says, 'and I'm gonna find you.'

Kat watches him. He hasn't looked on the porch yet. She doesn't know why – it doesn't make sense – but he hasn't. Not yet. She has no doubt that he will. Even if he doesn't, he's bound to see her movement in the corner of his eye while he looks elsewhere, and it will probably happen sooner rather than later. She can't just stand here leaning against the outside wall of her apartment; she has to get the apartment door opened without him seeing her. Once she does that, she can just let herself fall inside, kick the door shut, and, hopefully, if she's got any strength left, she'll be able to find enough in her to reach up and twist the dead-bolt home. And then she'll be safe.

But first, the door needs to be opened.

Easy-peasy, she thinks. It's already unlocked. All she has to do is turn the doorknob – without jingling the keys – and push the door open. That's all.

She reaches out with a raw shaking and bloody left hand. With her right hand, she grips onto the wall behind her, hoping she doesn't fall.

The man who attacked her is now out of sight in the courtyard; she can hear him cursing and stomping around.

She can do this. She just has to do it before he comes back out toward the street, that's all.

'Where are you, you bitch?'

She can do this.

Her fingers touch the cold metal of the key-scratched doorknob, and she reflexively pulls away, startled by the feeling.

Her nerves are shot.

Just do it, she tells herself. Before he comes back. Please, Kat, just do it.

She reaches out again, wraps her bloody hand around the doorknob.

She can hear the sound of his footsteps coming back.

She looks toward the courtyard. He is walking along the bloody trail she left behind on her way here. She dumbly thinks of Hansel and Gretel. There's something wrong with her brain. He is going to look up and see her soon. Any second now.

She can't worry about being quiet anymore.

She turns the doorknob, jingling the keys which stick from it as she does, and she shoves.

The door swings open and Kat falls with the momentum of her shove, face down on her front porch. She tries to scramble inside but she's so weak she can barely crawl, but she tries, and she manages to get the upper half of her body over the threshold and inside – I'm inside, she thinks, madly, I'm safe – before a hand grabs her by the leg and drags her back out into the early-morning darkness.

'No,' she screams, and the word tears at her throat like a jagged stone as it makes its way out of her. 'No.'

The man pulls her out and into a flower bed in front of the building with one hand, and with the other he brings the knife down. She twists as she tries to escape, and the blade stabs into her calf. And then another stab, this one into her left hip. She can feel the moist soil of the flower bed beneath her.

The sun hasn't come up, but there are no more stars in the sky.

Gray clouds swarm above her, blocking her view of anything beyond the atmosphere.

Something slides into her stomach.

31

David hasn't said a word; he's simply been sitting in the back of the ambulance, thinking.

He thinks of a boy with dark hair and light eyes – a small, pale boy – a boy who likes to sit in his bathtub, even when he's not taking a bath, and play with his toy cars, pretending the edge of the tub is a roadway, making the noise of a car shifting gear, but the car's going too fast, oh no, it's in trouble, it's gonna lose control, and then it does lose control and it flies off the road which is on a hundred-foot cliff, and it crashes to the bathroom rug below and explodes and the driver screams, 'Oh, no! My hair's on fire!' He thinks of a boy who tries to tell his father what happened to him at school, whose father calls him a liar, tells him not to make things up, tells him he's grounded for a week for making things up, tells him he's sick for even thinking up such things. He thinks of a boy who lies in bed afraid to go to school. A boy who stands in the bathroom, at the bathroom counter, grinding soap into his left eye, trying to give himself pinkeye, trying to give himself the appearance of pinkeye anyway, because pinkeye is contagious and they don't make you go to school when you have pinkeye, and when he's done his eye is red, so red it looks like it will never be white again, and for three days he gets to stay home with mom and listen to the radio and eat fried bologna sandwiches with the crust cut off. He thinks of a boy who's grounded for a month when he's caught grinding soap into his eye, giving himself pinkeye for the fourth time. A boy who packs a suitcase and runs away from home but who really only runs as far as the garage, who crawls up in the attic above the garage and sleeps there for four nights, only going into the house when his parents are gone, going into the house to collect cans of food and go to the bathroom. A boy who in that four days gathers quite a collection of piss-filled Mason jars in the garage attic. A boy who does nothing but sit and read *A Princess of Mars* by the dim light of the attic's sole window while his mom cries about her missing son. A boy who gets caught sneaking food from their General Electric Monitor Top refrigerator after his father pretends to leave but really hides just outside the kitchen, looking in through the window. A boy with welts from a razor strop who gets even more welts when his father finds the jars of piss in the attic and tells him he's disturbed, he's sick, making up lies about his teachers and saving his urine in jars. That's what he thinks of as they head toward the hospital, the monster he's wished dead for twenty-six years on a stretcher not a foot away, strapped down, unable to move, a jagged piece of glass sticking from his forehead like a shelf.

The ambulance pulls to a stop in front of the hospital.

The sirens go silent; the lights stop flashing.

He looks at Mr. Vacanti and the man looks back at him with somehow gentle eyes. It surprises David to see the man has gentle eyes. It surprises him, even at thirty-seven, to discover that monsters can have gentle eyes. Something is terribly wrong with a world where monsters are allowed to have gentle eyes.

'You're doing the right thing, Davey,' Mr. Vacanti says. 'What I did was . . . unforgivable. I know that. But you're doing the right thing.'

David clenches his jaw and looks away. He swallows back words. He turns toward the closed back doors of the ambulance, unlatches them, and forces them open.

He's surprised to see it's still dark out. It felt like he was in the ambulance for hours – days, weeks – with that monster and his gentle eyes.

With John's help, he pulls Mr. Vacanti out of the ambulance, and a moment later he and John take him into the hospital.

32

Diane sits on the bed beside a suitcase whose leather jaw is hinged open and whose mouth is full of her clothes, jewelry, memories.

She is holding a photograph in both hands, a framed wedding photograph, nineteen years old. In the photograph she and Larry are young and thin. Larry has all of his hair. None of her skin has begun to sag or wrinkle. Both of them have shining eyes: eyes that are shining with the youthful belief that love really can conquer all, and, worse to Diane as she looks at the picture now, that it actually has. Their eyes are shining with the belief that now they are safe. They are together and married and the world will never get to them. It might get to some people, but they're not some people. They're Larry and Diane.

They're safe.

There is a knock at the closed bedroom door.

Diane looks up from the photograph.

'I told you,' she says, 'I don't wanna talk to you and I can't stand to look at you.'

'Please, Diane,' Larry says in a muffled voice from the other side of the door, 'just let me come in.'

There is a rattle of doorknob, a futile shove. The door stands firm.

She looks down at the picture and wonders how either of them could ever have been so naive.

'I'm not letting you talk me into staying,' she says to the closed door.

'I don't want to talk you into anything. I just want to talk.'

'You don't want me to stay?'

'Of course I want you to stay. But this isn't about talking you into anything.' Silence, and then a very quiet, 'Fuck,' which is, of course, not intended for her; and then, 'Please. Open the door.'

Diane sets down the photograph, looks at it for a minute longer, and then tilts it down, pressing their smiling faces against the wood of the nightstand. She doesn't want to have to look at their goddamn innocent faces anymore.

'Diane?'

'What?'

'Please.'

God damn him.

She gets to her feet and walks to the door. She stares at it for a moment and then turns the lock and pulls it open.

Larry is standing there looking at her, a defeated man.

His eyes are red. What's left of his hair is a bird's nest. He's wearing no shirt, his flabby white belly simply hanging out, pale and vulnerable. There is desperation in his eyes, in his posture.

In their old life, Diane wouldn't have been able to stay mad at this broken Larry. The sight of him like this would have melted her heart. Her big strong Larry looking like a boy who's lost his dog. It would have gotten to her.

But this isn't their old life.

'I'm sorry,' he says.

'That's not good enough.'

Larry nods.

'I know. I know it's not. I know nothing is. But I love you and I don't want to lose you. I don't want that.'

'You're not losing me,' she says. 'You threw me away.'

'I didn't.'

'What do you call it? What do you call what you did? You made a promise, the most important promise a man can make to a woman, and then you broke that promise. You threw it away. What does that say about your feelings for me?'

'Nothing,' he says. 'It doesn't say a goddamn thing about my feelings for you.'

'I don't believe that.'

'It says I'm an idiot. It says that I don't appreciate what I've got until I'm threatened with losing it. It says I'm a bad person, a fuck up, a low life. Scum. But it doesn't say anything about my feelings for you, Diane. I love you. I will never stop loving you. If you can't forgive me and you have to leave, I understand that. It breaks my heart, but I understand that. But don't leave because you think my mistake means I don't love you. I want to continue to wake up next to you for the rest of my life, for the rest of our lives. I want you to know that. I've just been sitting out in the living room, trying to think of ways to tell you that, but there it is. I don't know how else to say it. I love you and I want us to stay together more than I've ever wanted anything. So if you're going to leave me, don't leave me because you think I don't love you, or I've thrown what we have away. If you can't forgive me, you can't. But I hope you can. I want you to. I'm asking you to. Please, Diane, forgive me. Please – forgive me and let me make it right again.'

Diane does not say anything for a long time. She stands there and she looks at Larry looking back at her with his pained red eyes. She thinks of the happy times when they met, and the several happy years that followed – but she also thinks of the sad years, their inability to have children, the miscarriages, the way it broke her heart, the way Larry blamed her as if she'd done it on purpose; she thinks of the way they can sit in the same room and seem miles apart, the silence between them.

'Diane?'

Diane shakes her head.

'I'm sorry,' she says. 'I just don't think I can.'

33

Harriette is tired – more tired than she has ever been before.

'Patrick.'

She does not say it loudly but Patrick is a good boy and attentive and a moment later the door is pushed open and he's standing there looking down on her with concern in his eyes.

'What is it, momma?'

'Why is it,' Harriette wonders aloud, 'that you can still call me momma, but I can't call you Pat anymore?'

Patrick smiles.

'That's different,' he says. 'Are you okay?'

It was hard – it was a hard life – raising him up alone for the last eight years and change, but looking at him now she thinks she's done all right.

'Of course I'm not okay, honey,' she says. 'I'm dying.'

Patrick does not say anything.

'I'm dying,' Harriette says again.

'Is there anything I can do?'

She holds up an orange bottle of pills in her hand.

'I couldn't get these opened.'

'It's not time for you to take your pills.'

Harriette nods her head and says, 'I believe it is, Patrick.'

She watches her son go pale as he comes to understand what she's saying; she watches him shake his head.

'Your arm,' he says, motioning to the machine in the corner, 'it didn't . . . you weren't in pain, were you?'

'I'm finished.'

'No.'

'Why not? I'm tired, Patrick. I'm tired and I'm bedridden and the only way I see the sun anymore is through a dirty pane of glass.'

She shakes her head.

She thinks of sleep, blissful darkness, the kind of blissful darkness she had before she was born. She felt no pain then. She felt nothing. She once heard life described as a brief window of light between two vast expanses of nothingness. She doesn't know if that's accurate – but she does know her light is flickering, and she hopes it's accurate: she wants it finished; she doesn't want to wake up ever again, not anywhere.

'I'm tired,' she says again.

Patrick walks over to her and reaches for the pills. She pulls her hand away, but he grabs her wrist and pries the bottle from her fingers.

'If you're tired,' he says, 'lay down and get some sleep.'

'I'm much more tired than that,' Harriette says. 'You're a young man. You don't understand yet what the world does to a person.'

'I can't let you—' He closes his eyes, just for a moment, but in that moment Harriette thinks her son looks beautiful, like his father used to look when she first met him. He's so like his father – only Patrick doesn't have the same rage. Henry was such an angry man. She's afraid that life will give that rage to Patrick too eventually – she thinks it will – but for now it's absent. He opens his eyes. 'I can't let you do what you want to do,' he says.

'Why?'

'I can stay. I won't report.'

'What good will you be in jail?'

'Then I'll report,' he says, 'but I'll tell them you're sick, that you're sick and you need me to stay to take care of you.'

'I want you to stop using me as an excuse, Patrick.'

'I don't know what you mean.'

'Yes, you do. You're a smart boy.'

'You asked me to take care of you.'

'Maybe I was wrong,' Harriette says, thinking the *maybe* is a kindness to herself she doesn't deserve. 'You're nineteen years old and the only life you live is through that damned telescope of yours. And I know you want more, Patrick. I know you do. But I also know you're afraid of . . . something. I don't know what. Maybe life itself. But you are and you're using me as an excuse. So stop. Stop using me as an excuse.'

Patrick looks to the corner. His eyes are bright and alive with emotion. After a while, he looks back. 'I'm not afraid of life,' he says. 'You're wrong about that, momma. I'm not afraid of the world.'

'What are you afraid of?'

'I'm afraid of . . .' He swallows and he has to look at his stocking feet to get it out. She understands that: sometimes you need to be alone to admit things to yourself – especially out loud. 'I'm afraid of becoming like him.'

'Your father.'

Patrick nods.

'Your father was not a good dad,' Harriette says. 'He was not a good husband. But he was not a bad man.'

'He . . . hurt me,' Patrick says. He looks away, blinks, and Harriette's heart breaks for the pain she sees inside him. But then it's gone. He swallows it and it's gone, replaced by coldness and something else.

That's when she's sure of it – when he gives her that cold look – that the world will, without a doubt, give Patrick the same rage that his father had in him, that he will not let himself hurt, and so the hurt will turn sour, and turn into something worse.

'I'm taking your pills with me so you don't do anything stupid,' he says, with no emotion in his voice. 'Get some sleep.'

34

Peter sits on the couch across from Bettie. He tilts the bottom of his tumbler toward the ceiling, washing the last of the whiskey and water and icemelt down his throat. A half-melted ice cube falls into his mouth as well – clattering against mercury-filled molars – but after swallowing the liquid, he spits it back into the glass and sets the glass down on his coaster on the coffee table. He stares at it. He thinks of the condensation ring in the bedroom. He doesn't understand how he can be thinking about that fucking ring when his life is falling apart, but he can – he is. He should take furniture polish to it. He also needs to scrub the whiskey out of the carpet.

He puts his right hand to his face, wipes at the corners of his mouth with index finger and thumb, and then takes his hand away again.

He stands up and sits down and stands up again.

'I have to talk to Anne.'

Bettie nods.

'You should do that.'

'I'm gonna go talk to Anne.'

He turns and walks away from Bettie. She is beautiful – and sexy in the same way he thinks Elizabeth Taylor is sexy – but he cannot believe he has put his marriage in jeopardy for that when he knows almost nothing about her. Her likes and dislikes. Whether she sleeps in on the weekends and does nothing till noon or if she wakes up bright and early and wants to get out of the house as soon as the sun rises. How she likes to spend her evenings. What kind of books she reads. Whether she reads books at all. He cannot believe he's endangered his marriage for a stranger with nice breasts and full lips. He is an idiot.

He grabs the doorknob and turns it and pushes his way into the bedroom.

When he does, Ron and Anne stop, and for a moment it's as if they are frozen. She is on her back on the bed, her ass to the edge of the mattress, and Ron is standing with his knees slightly bent, with Anne's ankles hooked over his shoulders, and he is inside of her. If it weren't so goddamn infuriating it would be a comical sight, but it's not a comical sight – not for Peter, not right now. He's on the verge of losing this woman, his wife, and there's a man, the man who started it all as far as he's concerned, who's taller than him, better looking than him, who seems like he knows his way around a car, who seems more confident and together, despite how hard Peter tries to hold himself together, to seem like he's got his shit in order, to project confidence – there's this motherfucker who probably would have beat him up in high school and he's got his dick in Peter's wife.

Ron pulls away from Anne and Anne sits up.

'Peter,' she says.

'I'll fucking kill you,' Peter says, spittle flying from his mouth, rage burning hot in his cheeks, chest aching as his heart pounds, and he feels like something ready to explode, like a bomb, and he leaps at Ron. His shoulder slams into Ron's naked stomach, shoving the man's back against the wall.

Peter swings with all his might, all his anger and rage, slamming his fist into Ron's chin. Ron's head whips to the left with the arc of the punch, but it doesn't give enough, and Peter feels his ring finger break at the impact – feels the knuckle give and then collapse into the rest of his hand, crumpling like an empty beer can. It shoots pain up his arm, an electric jolt up the hollows of his bones, but that only infuriates him more. As does the fact that Ron doesn't seem as hurt by the punch as Peter is himself. His hand is aching, on fire now, and Ron is simply turning back to Peter to look at him, is simply saying, 'Peter, you don't underst—' But Peter doesn't let him finish. He throws another punch, this time connecting with the nose, and the nose is soft, and he feels it bend beneath the force of his punch, under his aching fist, and then he feels something in Ron's nose snap like a dry twig – only the sound it makes isn't exactly dry – and he sees blood gush from Ron's face, run down his mouth, drip onto his naked chest and his slightly protruding belly. The man still has an erection. Unbelievable. And Ron wipes at the blood on his face with the back of his hand and says 'Peter' calmly – calmly, God damn him – 'I'm about to lose my patience.' Lose his patience? Peter wants him to fall to the ground, to fall down and beg for mercy. Peter wants to be the one who wins – just this once. He's putting everything he has into besting this man and the guy doesn't even notice it; the guy's simply about to lose his patience. The guy hasn't even tried to win yet, but Peter already knows it's inevitable. Because he's lost. But he tries one last punch anyway – one last punch. Ron simply catches it in his open hand, as if it were a tossed baseball, and shoves it away from its target, and with that the rage is gone, replaced by the knowledge of complete defeat. He has lost. He is not a man. If ever he had the potential to become one, even that potential is gone.

'Peter,' Anne says.

But he can't make eye contact. He is not a man and he does not deserve a woman – and Anne is a woman: a beautiful woman – and he has destroyed whatever it was that was keeping them together.

'I'm sorry,' Ron says.

'I'm not,' Anne says. 'You didn't care before Bettie rejected you.'

'I'm sorry,' Ron says again. 'The fun has been over for some time now, and I shouldn't have—'

'Can you please leave me and Anne alone?'

Peter looks up at Ron, who is covered in blood, who is dripping it onto the carpet, staining the carpet – who gives a fuck about the fucking carpet right now, Peter? – and Ron nods his head.

'Okay.'

'Thank you,' Peter says.

Ron walks toward the door looking back at Peter and Anne, and there's something like pity in his eyes when he looks at Anne, and Peter feels anger heavy in his gut again like a hot stone – that son of a bitch – but then the guy is out the door, shutting it quietly behind him.

Peter looks at his wife, looks into her eyes. They are sad and pained and angry all at once. How can he ever make her understand that it was all just idiocy on his part and that he knows it was – that a lot of it was simply wanting to have something that belonged to Ron, a man who represents everything he believes he's not, and that he didn't even know that's what it was until right now? How can he tell her that it was all because he's weak and effeminate and has small hands and thin wrists and for once he just wanted to take something away from one of the guys who've been taking away his dignity all of his life, with their snide comments, with their condescension, with the way they try to rip him off when he takes his car to the mechanic or when he calls the plumber, knowing that he doesn't know enough about those things to stand up for himself? He wants to tell her about how small he feels when that happens.

When guys just like Ron take his barstool when he walks away to take a leak, simply shove his beer aside, and when he comes back they act like he's not even there or like he's inconveniencing them when he reaches past to get his bottle. When guys like Larry across the courtyard come over – come over because he invited him and his wife over, because Peter has always wanted to be one of the guys even though he's never felt like he was; he's always felt like he was standing outside that group looking in; and Larry is nothing if not one of the guys – and chide him for not knowing how to cook a steak like a man. Like a man? It's my goddamn kitchen and I'll cook a steak any goddamn way I please, Larry, you son of a bitch, and if I want a fucking red wine and cranberry sauce on it, that's what I'll have.

He can't tell her any of that, can he? Because men cannot be weak. Men cannot be confused. Men cannot feel small and alone and pathetic. He cannot tell her that, but he has to tell her something. He has to tell her something, anything – anything but that.

'Anne,' he says.

'Peter.'

He licks his lips.

'Anne,' he says.

35

Lying on her back Kat can see the first touches of morning light in the sky as the sun, not yet visible, begins to bleach morning into existence from the other side of the horizon, and the light reveals how dark and ugly the clouds are overhead. Dark and gray and ugly and mean.

To see the sky she has to look past the sweating, cruel face which is hovering only inches from hers, wearing a grimace, the eyes bloodshot and cold and desperate. Her body is being ground down into the moist soil under her back, and she can feel the man's thing inside her, tearing her, and she knows she must be bleeding down there now, too. She just wants it to be over. She wants it to be over and she can smell his hot breath on her face – food and digestion and an abscessed tooth.

Both of the man's hands are gripping at her shoulders, the fingers digging into her flesh. She thinks she can feel one of the fingers inside the hole where he stabbed her –

behind the collarbone in her right shoulder – but she hurts so bad everywhere now, she is so cold and numb and pained simultaneously, that she's not sure. She's not sure of anything but the gray clouds gathering overhead and the bloodshot eyes of the man on top of her.

And the hands gripping her shoulders.

Gripping her shoulders, not gripping the knife.

The knife. With rust flecks like freckles.

It must be somewhere.

Forget where you are, Kat, forget where you are and close your eyes and feel for the knife, for the cold of the metal.

Find the knife.

It must be somewhere.

Kat closes her eyes so she doesn't have to look at the man's face. She closes her eyes and she reaches out with her hands, feeling for the knife, praying to God that she finds it – please, God, I've tried to be good and I don't know why you're punishing me, but I've tried to be good, so please, please, please won't you just let me find the knife, please – and she feels the black dirt, and she can smell manure in the soil, and her hand touches something, but it's just the stem of a flower; and then she feels something else, she thinks she feels something else, and then the very tip of the knife stabs into her finger – the tip of the knife not the thorn on a rose; she's sure of it; there are no roses here – and there's a little bit of pain, but she can barely feel it and she's glad for it because it means she found the knife.

She found it. It's right there. She tries to grab it but she only pushes it away. She accidently pushes it away or spins it slightly out of her reach, and she tries to stretch to grab it, but now it's gone. It seems to be gone, but it can't be gone. It's right there.

Where did it go?

Where could it have gone?

It was right there a second ago.

'Oh, God, you bitch,' the man on top of her says, and she can feel him building to a climax, and she hurts down there. He's tearing her down there.

She opens her eyes and his face is only inches from hers, and sweat is beading on it and dripping from it, and his eyes are bloodshot and cold and desperate.

And she sees the knife now, in the corner of her eye. The man grabbed it, grabbed it from the soil; he grabbed it and he is holding it. She can see it in the corner of her eye.

She feels the man spasm inside her, and she wants to be sick – it makes her sick inside; it makes her feel like her insides have gone rotten; he's made her rotten inside – and if she ever gets out of this she's going to scrub inside herself with bleach, with hot water and bleach, until she feels clean again, if she ever can feel clean again.

'You cunt,' he says.

He thrusts himself into her and pushes his upper body away from her.

He spasms again, and he brings the blade down into her chest, and she hears a pop – it pops as it breaks through her breastbone – and pain shoots outward, explodes outward, and her chest is on fire, and the fire spreads to every other part of her body, and she screams but the scream is silent. She can't even scream out loud anymore, but the sound still fills her head, her aching, echoing head.

And when she looks toward the sky, toward the gathering gray clouds, when she looks toward the sky and God, to ask why, all she sees are the bloodshot eyes in the face in front of her. The eyes of the man with the knife. They go wide as she looks into them, those eyes, and then suddenly they're not cold anymore; they go wide and scared and soft.

'I'm . . . oh, my God,' the man says.

He says that and he falls away from her. He scrambles to his feet, and he looks down on her with wide, terrified eyes.

'Oh, my God,' he says again.

He wipes at his eyes.

'I'm sorry,' he says, and then he turns and he runs away from there.

She can hear his footsteps thumping away, the sound of his big construction boots pounding against concrete. Then she hears a car door squeak open and slam shut. She hears the loose, jangly sound of his car's engine starting. She sees, in the corner of her eye, the splash of headlights against the oak trees growing in front of the Hobart Apartments. She hears the sound of the car driving away, and the splash of the headlights is gone.

Kat feels like she is drowning.

She looks down at her chest and she can see the wood handle of the kitchen knife sticking out of it. She can see the handle throbbing with the beat of her heart as if the knife itself had a pulse.

If God wanted her dead this badly, He could have at least made it quick – made it quick and painless – He didn't have to make it torture.

'Fuck you, God,' she says to the gathering gray clouds above her. 'Fuck you,' she says. 'I'm not going to die.'

36

Frank sits in the back seat of the police cruiser, hands cuffed behind his back – cuffed tightly, so that the flow of blood is cut off.

His fingertips are going numb. Blood drips down from an egg-shaped lump on his forehead. He can see several cops digging through his trunk. There are now three more police cars parked on the side of the road, and half a dozen cops, most of whom appear to have nothing to do, wandering about like lost puppies.

Frank watches Kees walk up to one of them and say something but he cannot hear what he says and it probably doesn't matter; the other cop nods and Kees turns away, walks toward his cruiser with Frank inside, pulls open the driver's side door, and falls into his seat.

Pulling the door shut behind him, Kees looks back at Frank over his shoulder with a second lieutenant smirk on his smug face. There is crusted blood in his right ear.

'You still think you're smarter than me?'

'I think most houseplants are smarter than you.'

This guy's gonna do what he's gonna do; he's doing it; pretending respect at this point serves no purpose. He's framing Frank whether he calls him *sir* or not, so fuck him.

The smirk vanishes.

'You still haven't learned your lesson, huh?'

'I've learned a lot of lessons, son,' Frank says. 'I'm not a young man.'

'And I'm not your son.'

Kees turns back around, starts the cruiser, puts it in gear. Then puts it back in park, and looks back over his shoulder.

'If you're so smart, what the fuck are you doing in the back of my car with your hands cuffed?'

'I didn't say anything about myself,' Frank says. 'I said you were an idiot. Anyone who thinks they can't be touched is bound to get hit the hardest; they won't have their guard up when it finally comes down.'

Kees makes a face like someone made him suck a lemon and turns around. He puts the car in gear and pulls it out into the street.

'You don't know shit,' Kees tells him. 'You think you do but you don't.' He looks at Frank in the rearview mirror and Frank looks back. 'I'll tell you something about the way the world works, old man. In this world,' he says, 'you're either the teeth or the throat they sink into, and there ain't no in between.'

Frank thinks Kees might be right to a point. But then there's always a bigger set of teeth, isn't there? And that's what he hasn't learned yet. The seal might eat the little fish – but the shark eats the seal. Frank has learned it, though. He's learned it because he's been bitten many times in his life. And now he's been bitten again. He just hopes this bite doesn't end him; he'd like to see his wife again without bars between them.

The police cruiser pulls up to the station and comes to a stop. Kees steps from the car, walks around to the back, pulls open the door, and tries to yank Frank out bodily. Frank is a big man, though, and Kees's hand simply slips away from Frank's t-shirt.

Frank looks up at the man, waiting.

'Get out of the car,' Kees says.

Frank does, he steps from the car, and Kees pushes him forward toward the police station. Frank glances at the man over his shoulder as he walks toward the station, and the guy's got an expression on his face like a fisherman who's landed a big one; Frank's hands clench behind his back, forming fists.

Kees shoves Frank inside.

He's trying to think of a way out of this mess. The guy planted enough evidence on him to make him look guilty no matter what he says. He doesn't want to go to prison. If he had to be locked up in order to avoid the same happening to Erin, if that were the case, he'd go willingly. He wouldn't like it but he'd do it – and willingly. But that's not the case. Erin killed no one. She simply ran over a child's toy with her car – a stroller with a doll inside. That's all. And that's not a crime. He doesn't want to go to prison, but he can't think of how to get out of it. But he's already decided once they get him in the interrogation room he's not talking. He might have already talked too much. He's not talking because he doesn't want to tell the cops why he was where he was in the first place. Doesn't matter that a baby in a stroller wasn't hit and killed. He doesn't want to tell them and he won't. He doesn't want to tell them anything. He knows cops. They can find ways to put innocent statements in a context that makes them sound terrible – in a context that can convince a jury to convict a man. Especially a colored man. Frank might be going to prison, but he'll be damned if he's gonna help this son of a bitch put him there.

As Kees pushes Frank through the station, an older man in a cheap suit that's wearing out at the elbows – whose face is seamed together with wrinkles, whose gray hair looks heavy and flat and unhealthy and brittle, whose nose is a burst of broken capillaries and covered in blackheads – walks over to Kees and grabs him by the arm, not gently.

'Let's take a walk to my office,' the guy says.

'With all due respect, sir,' Kees says, his tone suggesting

the amount of respect due is exactly none, 'I've got a suspect in custody.'

Sir, Frank thinks, despite the tone. Sir: someone more important than him – someone with bigger teeth.

'Did I ask you what you were doing?' the guy in the suit says. 'Did I? Because I don't remember doing that.'

'No, sir.'

'If I didn't ask, why are you telling me?'

'I'm just saying, sir,' Kees says, and now there's a hesitation in his voice, 'that I think . . . our conversation . . . can wait?'

'Well, I don't give a good goddamn what you think, Officer Kees. What you think doesn't matter. What I think is what matters. See, this is a hierarchy, and you're at the bottom.'

Kees says nothing for a long time. Then: 'Yes, sir.' Then: 'What do you want me to do with the suspect?'

The guy in the suit looks at Frank, nods his head at him.

Frank nods back.

'Mr. Riva,' the guy in the suit says, 'can join us in my office.'

Now Kees's face goes pale and takes on a greenish tint.

Apparently, Frank thinks, this is not standard operating procedure.

'Sir?'

'Let's go.'

*

Frank is escorted into a small room, maybe twelve by ten, that smells of wet plaster, mold, and whiskey sweat. He sees by walnut slab and engraved brass plate on the desk that the guy in the suit has a name, and it's Captain Busey. Pretty convenient that his mother named him Captain, Frank thinks.

There is already a man in the room, sitting, facing the desk, his back to the door. There is white gauze wrapped around his head. Red blood has seeped through and dried to burgundy.

Busey reaches into his pocket and pulls out a wad of keys and uncuffs Frank.

'Sir,' Kees says.

'No.' Then Busey looks at Frank. 'Have a seat, Mr. Riva.'

Frank nods.

'Thank you, sir.'

He walks to a chair that sits to the left of the man with the gauze on his head. The guy looks at him from the corner of his eye and nods a greeting. Frank nods back thinking this poor bastard sure took a worse beating than he did. His entire head is wrapped in gauze and the lower left half of his face is one enormous purple bruise that has split open and is leaking a thick clear liquid about the consistency and color of aloe juice, red floating in the liquid like it's a fertilized chicken egg. His mouth is slightly open and Frank can see what's left of his teeth: little jagged pieces of them sticking from his bloody gums like shards of glass left in a window frame when the window's been shattered. A little bit of blood starts to drip out of his mouth over his teeth shards. The guy makes a liquid sucking sound and the blood disappears.

O God, smash their teeth in their mouth.

Frank looks away.

Behind him Kees says, 'What's going on, sir?'

'You mean why am I here when I should be home in bed beside my warm wife and beneath my comfortable blankets? Why don't you ask Mr. Reynolds that question, Kees, since he knows the story better than I do?'

Frank looks over his shoulder at Kees and sees that he's looking even sicker. He simply stares at the back of the gauze-covered head next to Frank. Frank can see the wheels spinning behind his eyes.

'I don't know what this man told you, sir, but whatever it is, it's not true.'

'You don't know what he said, but he's lying?' Busey shakes his head. 'Sit down, Officer Kees.'

'Sir.'

'Sit the fuck down!'

Kees does not respond to that, apparently thinks the time for talking might be over. He walks to the last empty chair – save Busey's – which is just to the right of the guy Busey called Mr. Reynolds, and he sits down.

'Mr. Reynolds,' Busey says, 'have you ever seen Mr. Riva before?'

Mr. Reynolds looks at Frank. More blood starts to drip

from his mouth and he sucks it back in. Frank avoids cringing, but a brief tic afflicts his right eye, the tense muscle there having an anxious spasm.

'No, sir,' Mr. Reynolds says, the words sounding wet somehow. 'I have not.'

'This man received serious head trauma, sir,' Kees says. 'He has no idea what he's saying. I've never even seen him before. I don't—'

'Shut your fucking mouth, Kees.' Busey shakes his head. 'You have caused me far more trouble than you're worth.'

Busey walks to the black fabric chair behind his desk. Frank can see a dark triangle in the middle of the chair's back where Busey has sweated into it, and white flakes on the arms of the chair that he thinks are fallen bits of deodorant powder or dandruff or both. Then Busey sits. A sigh escapes his mouth. He puts his elbows on his desk – something he must do often, as there are two areas on the desk's surface that have had the finish rubbed away – and puts his face into his open palms. He rubs his face. His callused hands against beard stubble make a sound like sandpaper. He snorts the liquid out of his nose, into the back of his throat, and swallows.

He looks up at Frank and Mr. Reynolds.

Franks waits.

'Being a police officer on the streets of this city is a stressful job,' Busey says. 'I'm not excusing what Officer Kees did, understand; I'm simply saying that sometimes good men snap and do bad, or stupid, things.' It already sounds like a rehearsed speech to Frank and he wonders if Busey stood in the bathroom, staring into the water-spotted mirror, practicing, some guy grunting out his last meal in a toilet stall behind him. Frank would bet yes; he'd bet green money on it. 'What officer Kees did,' Busey continues, 'was both. Stress gets to a person; sometimes the streets can turn a good smart man simple and violent. Recently there was some trouble related to a Negro protest. Some people got hurt who maybe shouldn't have. One young man got killed. You might have read about it in the papers. If what happened tonight gets out, combined with what happened at that Negro protest – well, it will undermine the credibility of the department. You're both law-abiding citizens, good citizens. You have jobs, you pay your taxes, you vote. You're the kind of people who know that a compromised police department cannot do its job, that a police department needs the faith of the public in order to operate. The kind of people who understand that police business is important business. The kind of people who know and understand that this city is dangerous and the police department needs to be able to do its job.'

Busey licks his lips.

Frank hears a liquid sucking sound coming from his right.

Kees is silent.

Frank looks down at his hands – laced together, resting in his lap – and then back up at Busey. He's still waiting –

waiting for the punchline. Most people don't start a joke without one in mind.

'Okay, then,' Busey says. He looks down at a couple sheets of paper that are sitting on his desk between his elbows, then he picks them up and hands one to Frank and one to Mr. Reynolds. Frank looks at his.

'I am prepared,' Busey says, 'to offer you both a significant cash settlement if you're willing to sign this agreement saying that the department is not at fault and that you will make nothing that happened tonight a matter of public record. How does that sound?'

'How significant?' Mr. Reynolds says, followed by the liquid sucking sound, which is, itself, followed by the sound of swallowing. Frank imagines eating a raw egg.

Busey writes a number on a piece of paper and slides it across the desk.

'That applies to both of you.'

Frank and Mr. Reynolds look at it.

Then Mr. Reynolds looks up. 'It doesn't seem fair,' liquid suck, 'that we get the same amount,' liquid suck, 'when I'm,' liquid suck, 'in so much worse shape.'

Busey purses his lips and whistles between his teeth, presses his palms together, touches them to his chin, and then takes them apart again.

'Okay,' he says, finally. 'Add fifty percent.'

Mr. Reynolds nods.

'Okay,' he says.

Busey smiles.

'That's what I like to hear. Good man. Mr. Riva?'

Frank doesn't answer for a long time. He simply stares at the sheet of paper with the blue-ink number scrawled across it.

'What's going to happen to Officer Kees?'

'He'll be reprimanded and receive a two-week suspension.'

'With pay?'

Busey nods. 'Most likely.'

'So his punishment,' Frank says, 'is a paid vacation. This motherfucker tried to kill a man, and he tried to frame me for it, and you're saying in two weeks he'll be back on the streets dressed in blue? He should be in prison, not putting other people there.'

Ten minutes ago Frank thought he was going to prison. Now he knows he's not, and part of him thinks he should just be glad he's getting out of this at all, but he's not. He's not glad. He's furious. He's known the world is broken for a long time, he's known that, but sometimes he's amazed at how broken; even now, at this point in his life, nearing fifty years old, he can stumble across something that makes him realize all over again that the world is not only broken, but beyond fixing. No amount of glue can ever make it right. And yet, you have to focus on your little part of it, don't you? You have to focus on your little corner of the world and glue what cracks you can. Otherwise there's no hope at all.

Captain Busey is saying, 'A black mark on an officer's record is a serious matter, Mr. Riva. A *serious* matter.'

'As serious as murder?'

Busey sighs – an exasperated father.

'I can appreciate your point of view,' he says, 'and I can even understand why it's going to be hard for you to sign that agreement, monetary benefits notwithstanding. But,' Busey says, leaning forward on his elbows, glaring with creepily-light gray eyes, bloodshot and yellow at the corners, 'you will sign, Mr. Riva. It's no longer a request.'

'And if I don't?'

Busey shrugs.

'We've got a stolen TV with your fingerprints all over it.' He scratches his cheek. 'And while I don't know Mr. Reynolds very well, I'm betting it wouldn't take much to get him to testify against you. Your share of the money, say. And let me tell you something, Mr. Riva. We're gonna keep that evidence for a long time, and it's gonna have your name on it. I'm gonna keep it close to me, and you're gonna keep your mouth shut.'

Frank feels his jaw go tight.

He looks at the agreement clenched in his hand. He looks at the blue-inked number sitting on Busey's desk.

The world is just broken; that's all there is to it. You glue together the cracks you can but you don't let yourself fall through the ones you can't. Not if you can help it. It won't do you any good and chances are it won't do anybody else any good either.

Frank grabs a pen, leans to the desk, signs the agreement, and flings it toward Busey. Then he gets to his feet.

'I don't want your money.'

'Even better,' Busey says.

'I'd like to go home now.'

'Drive him home, Officer Kees. Your suspension is effective upon your return.'

'I'd prefer if it was someone else,' Frank says.

'Drive him home, Officer Kees.'

37

William pulls the station wagon up to the closed garage door with the dent in it. He kills the engine.

He looks at himself in his rearview mirror. Blood is smeared across his cheek. His eyes are vacant and shell-shocked.

He told himself it wouldn't happen again but it has. It has happened again.

He pushes open the driver's side door and steps out.

Elaine will be mad that he lost the kitchen knife; he'll have to think up a story about it. Maybe he'll tell her that he couldn't find a screwdriver and used the tip to try to unscrew something – he'll think of what later: maybe he dropped his lighter into the floor vent and needed to take the grate off to get to it, maybe something else – and it snapped off, so he threw it away. Yes. That's what he'll tell her when she asks about the knife. He'll say they need a new set of kitchen knives anyway. These ones have begun to get rust spots on them – stainless steel my ass, he'll say.

He can't believe it happened again.

It's Elaine's fault for shoving him away. The girl would have lived if he hadn't gone back, and if Elaine hadn't pushed him away, he wouldn't have. He probably wouldn't have.

How did he become this person he is?

He hates himself.

He walks up the path to his front door, and pushes his way inside. He walks directly to the bathroom. He has blood and dirt under his fingernails. His sweater has large sticky stains of drying blood on it. The fabric is dark, so you can't tell it's blood, but it is. The knees of his jeans are still moist from the soil in the flower bed and particles of dirt are ground into the weave of the fabric.

He undresses and looks at himself in the mirror. He does not like what he sees.

He steps into the shower and turns on the water.

38

David steps out of the diner carrying a greasy brown paper bag. The diner opens at five o'clock in the morning and is one of a few decent places he and John like to grab a bite at this hour. There's also an all-night diner not far from here but the food there is made for drunks who can't taste anything weaker than a ninety proof.

The first time David tried to order two cheeseburgers here, the lady behind the counter – he found out later her name was Annette – looked at him like he was crazy. 'How about a couple eggs over easy and some hash browns?' she said. But that was breakfast food, and he'd already eaten breakfast. He ate it at nine o'clock the night before. After five minutes he'd managed to convince her that he really did want two cheeseburgers, and also some onion rings. Two orders. Annette went to the window between the front and the kitchen, talked to the cook in hushed tones – as if they were discussing state secrets – and came back. She told him it would have to be cheeseburgers and fries, no onion rings, but otherwise it was all right. So burgers and fries it was and burgers and fries it is. When he walks through the door these days Annette greets him by name. The food is good and he doesn't have to deal with the swaying depressives putting off alcoholic fumes that the all-night joints always seem to attract. He doesn't like to see those guys – it's like looking into a mirror that reflects the future rather than the present. He can barely face today; he wants nothing to do with tomorrow, not till it's here – and probably not then either.

He glances up at the gathering gray clouds and pulls open the door. Inside the ambulance, he sees that John's already pulled out the ice chest and is drinking his first beer. They usually share a six pack with dinner. He pulls the door closed behind him.

He digs through the greasy paper bag and pulls out John's cheeseburger, which is wrapped in yellow paper smeared with mayonnaise. He hands it to him, as well as his little paper tray of fries. Then he grabs a Schlitz from the ice chest between their seats, peels off the top, and tosses the metal tab aside. He takes a swallow. It tastes good; after three, and maybe another sip or two from his flask, he might just start to feel human.

He burps and then goes to work on his burger. He's starved.

'You haven't said much since we dropped that guy off,'

John says through a mouthful of pink ground beef and American cheese.

'I haven't had much to say.'

'What did he do to you?'

David shrugs. 'The details don't matter. They never do.'

They eat silently for a while, taking occasional swallows from their beers, dipping fries into smears of ketchup loaded into the corners of their paper trays, wiping greasy fingers on their pants, burping, and eating some more.

'But you wanted him dead,' John says after a while.

David drains his beer, tosses the tin can into the ice chest, grabs a fresh one, and opens it. He washes some soggy potato and some soggier bread down his throat with it, looks out into the dull-colored morning.

'I'm not finished with him,' he says. 'Not even close.'

39

Thomas steps out of the shower, grabbing a towel from a rod as he does, and wiping himself dry with it. It's the same towel he's used since the last time he did laundry over a week ago and it's beginning to smell a bit sour. Dead skin clinging to a towel doesn't smell good even if it's clean dead skin. After he's dry he hangs the towel back on the rod and grabs a pair of clean underwear he set out on the toilet seat. He steps into them and out of the bathroom, trailed by a cloud of swirling steam.

He walks to the closet and slides the door open. He grabs a pair of blue-gray pants with a black stripe running down the outside seam and steps into them. He thinks about last night. He thinks about Christopher who is standing at the bedroom window looking out. He grabs a folded undershirt from the closet shelf and slips into it. It's inside-out but that doesn't matter. He pulls a light blue United States Postal Service shirt from a hanger and slips his arms into it. He turns away from the closet buttoning the shirt and looks at Christopher. The early-morning light is shining through the window and onto his face.

'What are you looking at?' Thomas says, finishing the last button.

Christopher looks at Thomas, then looks back to the window, through the window.

'I don't think anyone called the police,' he says.

'Oh, God,' Thomas says, remembering that shadow of a woman out there last night. 'I think you're right. We would have seen the lights or heard sirens or something. Is she still out there?'

Christopher shakes his head.

'No,' he says. 'I don't see her, anyway. But look.'

Thomas suddenly gets a knot in his stomach. He realizes he doesn't want to look. He realizes he's not going to like what he sees. He doesn't have to see it to know he won't like it.

He walks slowly to the window, looking at Christopher's face as he does, trying to find out what's outside by reading his expression, trying to prepare himself.

But then he's at the window and he looks out.

Something terrible has happened; they have let something terrible happen.

The courtyard is now completely visible, the outside lamps still on, the morning light beginning to fill what shadows they do not. The sun is still not yet visible above the horizon, but it has managed to bleach the sky a dirty white color, the gray clouds rumbling around up there, loitering, looking for trouble.

There is a pool of blood near the courtyard entrance by Austin Street. A trail leading to one of the benches in the courtyard. The bench is splattered with blood and there is another pool of it just a foot away on the concrete – enough blood there, Thomas thinks, for a rodent to drown in. There are a few women's bloody footprints, but most of the footprints – and there are dozens of them – are man sized, the angry stomps of a man on the hunt. Then there's the bloody trail of handprints leading from the bench, around the corner, to the front, the path accented by various smears and hash marks. Someone on hand and knee, attempting an escape.

The courtyard is simply a canvas on which the horror of the night has been painted. Thomas has never seen so much blood in his life.

40

The reason Christopher didn't see Kat is because she's around the corner, on the Austin Street-side of the building, but she's still out there on her hands and knees, dripping blood, trying to get to her apartment. The knife is still in her chest, throbbing as if it had its own pulse, throbbing like a thumb that's been smashed with a hammer. And she is trying not to slip on her own blood as she crawls. Trying not to slip because if she does she'll fall on the knife and send it deeper into her chest.

She feels like she's drowning.

She feels an itch in her throat, which makes her cough – choke, gag – and a long flow of liquid oozes from inside her, a long string of congealed blood.

She's bleeding into herself. She believes she is drowning in her own blood.

She is cold everywhere.

How many hours and hours and hours must have

passed? She can't imagine. It feels like it's been days – she feels like she must have missed half a dozen sunsets and sunrises. She knows it's not true; she would have seen people if that were true – people going to work and coming home from work, people checking their mail, people driving by on the street, people parking in the Long Island Railroad parking lot across the street – and one of them surely would have helped her. It can't have been days but it feels like it must have been. She imagines herself here motionless while people dart around her as if in timelapse footage, moving here and there, faster than is humanly possibly, getting into and out of cars, coming home with groceries, taking out trash, the sun rising and setting in mere moments, clouds forming and breaking apart again, flowers opening and closing and dying. She imagines herself here motionless while the world moves on around her. Then she imagines herself gone.

She moves a hand forward and it slips and she barely manages to keep herself up with her other three limbs.

She tries again and this time she manages to move herself forward.

Just a bit. Just a little bit.

I'm not going to die, she thinks.

She looks down at her bloody hands, at the dirt now under her fingernails, at the blood dripping between them, dripping from the handle of the knife in her chest, and then she looks up to the three feet or so to the open door. Open door. At least she got it open again. Three feet.

Six inches each step she takes, three feet away. First the doorway, then the phone. Just think about the doorway for now. Six inches each step, six steps to go.

Six. She's not going to die.

She moves herself forward another step, on hand and knee. The world goes gray, black dots swim in the air before her eyes – like insects, like dust motes – and she fights to stay conscious.

She is not going to die out here. She can do this.

He's not going to come back again.

Don't think about the phone.

Just get to the doorway.

Just get to the doorway.

Just get to the doorway.

41

William pours two cups of coffee and then sets the electric Sunbeam percolator down on the counter. He is dressed in clean jeans and a clean plaid work shirt. After his shower he got a trash bag and stuffed his bloody clothes – pants and sweater – into it and tied it up and hid it at the bottom of the trash can, lifting out some cracked egg shells and old newspapers first, and then replacing them atop the bag of clothes.

Next time Elaine does laundry she will find out they're missing. She might ask him about them but by then he'll have thought of something, a reason they're missing. He can't think of anything right now but it's been a long night.

Elaine morning-stumbles to the kitchen doorway wearing the robe William's mom got her for Christmas last year. She leans against the doorway, hugging herself.

William picks up both cups of coffee, walks one to Elaine, and hands it to her.

'Good morning,' he says.

She sips her coffee.

He sips his. It's good – hot and bitter and good. Gentle steam rises from their mugs and dissipates.

'Where did you go last night?' she says after a while.

'I went for a walk.'

Elaine shakes her head.

'That's not the truth.'

William looks away; he can't look at her.

'I did something bad.'

'What did you do?'

'I don't . . .'

'What did you do?'

He swallows.

'I hurt someone.'

'What happened?'

'I hurt someone.'

He looks at his wife.

She is a heavy woman. She wasn't when they met – she used to be thin and beautiful – but time does things to people and now she is heavy. William doesn't really mind. She is also a sweet woman, a good wife. He doesn't know how he ended up with her. He can't let her know what he is. She'll pack her things and she'll take the kids and she'll go away and she'll never come back. That's what'll happen if she finds out. He can't let her know what he is – but part of him wants to. Part of him wants it out in the open, exposed, over with.

He sets his coffee down on the counter and reaches into his front breast pocket. He pulls out his cigarettes and lighter, sticks a cigarette between his lips and starts a fire.

He can't let her know what he is but part of him wants to.

'I have these . . .'

He takes a deep drag on his cigarette – feels the smoke swim in his porous lungs, warm and heavy as liquid – and exhales through his nose. He looks at the clock on the wall. It's almost five forty, twenty minutes to six.

'I have to get to work,' he says.

He downs the rest of his coffee in three big swallows, burps, pauses, and takes a drag off his cigarette.

He told himself this wouldn't happen again but it has.

He walks to Elaine and kisses her cheek; she does not turn her head toward him to accept it.

'I have to get to work,' he says again, then heads toward the front door. He grabs the doorknob, pulls the door open and steps through, out into the morning light.

He simply stands on the front porch for a minute, smoking and looking out at this new day. New day, yes, but it's the same old world.

He feels shaky and weak from his lack of sleep. His eyes burn.

It's Elaine's fault. If she hadn't pushed him away it never would have happened. He wouldn't have gone back.

Elaine opens the door behind him and looks out at him. He turns around, startled.

'What happened last night?' She looks down at his feet. 'Is that blood on your boots? It looks like blood on your boots.'

He looks down at them, his boots, and sees the faded smudges from where he scrubbed them earlier, and sees new bloodstains on top of those. Those ones he didn't wash. The new ones he didn't wash. He doesn't know why he didn't wash the new stains; he should have.

He can't tell her. Part of him wants to.

He can't tell anyone.

'I'm gonna be late,' he says, and walks to the car.

42

Patrick has made up his mind. He walks to mom's bedroom and pushes open the door, knocking lightly as he does – hello, I'm here – and steps in.

Mom is sitting up in bed, looking out at the gray morning.

'You're up,' he says.

'I never went to sleep.'

'I thought you were tired.'

'I already said it's the kind of tired sleep can't fix.'

Patrick nods.

'I've been thinking about that,' he says. 'I've just been thinking about that and I was thinking about getting drafted, thinking about going off to war, thinking about traveling to Vietnam and killing people who never did anything to me, maybe getting killed myself. It scares me when I think about it. But if I don't go . . .' If he doesn't go, it will be because his mother is sick and he has to take care of her, because he has to stay here and take care of her until she dies; otherwise he must go. He did not receive a request to report for a physical examination; he received an Order to Report. Either they allow him to stay because his mother is sick or he goes. The alternative is jail, and he isn't going to go from one small room to another, smaller, room. He lets out a sigh, shakes his head. 'If you really want to go, if you mean it, if you're really finished – I'll help you. But I'll also stay if you want me to, if the army will let me.'

Mom stares at him for a long time through the folds of skin that surround her eyes. She doesn't move; she just looks at him. He feels as if she is trying to figure out something by looking at him but he has no idea what. Then she nods.

'Thank you,' she says.

43

Frank is in the front passenger seat of the police cruiser, looking through the spotted glass of the window, clenching and unclenching his jaw and just wanting to be away from this motherfucker.

'It wasn't personal,' Kees says, breaking the silence.

'It wasn't personal to you. It was pretty goddamn personal to me. You tried to put me in prison. Would have ruined not only my life, but my wife's. And I happen to love my wife.'

'Just doing what I had to do.'

'Oh, bullshit.'

'You don't know what I go through.'

'Well, let's all shed a fucking tear for the homicidal policeman,' Frank says, laughing angrily. 'I don't know what you go through? I don't need to know. I know you tried to kill a man and your boss just lickity-split cleaned up an attempted murder with some of the department's petty cash. I don't know what you go through? Motherfucker, you're the one that don't live in reality. You got that blue on, it's like a shield. The rest of us gotta walk through the city naked.'

'This uniform isn't a shield,' Alan says, shaking his head. 'It's a target.'

'Maybe it's not the uniform that's the target. Maybe it's you. In fact, I'm fucking sure of it.'

Frank is breathing hard now and his cheeks feel hot and his hands are balled into fists. He's as angry as he can remember being. He can feel the tendons tight in his arms. Tight with tension. And in his neck. And he feels a throbbing in his temples. He's more than just angry at the cop sitting next to him; he's angry at the world that has allowed him to exist, that has encouraged his existence. No wonder he can walk around with that second lieutenant smirk on his face doing whatever the hell he goddamn pleases – the world is made for assholes like him. Frank has always believed that people like him get what they deserve in the end but he doesn't believe that anymore. Not now, not ever again. He unballs his fists and balls them up again. He feels an ache in his tight knuckles, a spring-loaded tension in his forearms.

'If you weren't wearing that uniform I would fuck you up for what you tried to do to me.'

As the words leave Frank's mouth, Kees turns the wheel to the right and brings the cruiser to a stop by the curbside in front of the Hobart Apartments.

He looks at Frank and smiles.

'Then why don't we just pretend I'm *not* wearing the uniform, Frank?'

'For the same reason I don't pretend the ground is made out of marshmallows and jump off buildings. I don't need reality slamming me in the face. The world hits you hard enough when you take it for what it is.'

Kees licks his lips, doesn't look away from him.

'I won't tell if you don't.'

Frank knows he's bluffing, knows it because he's wearing that goddamn second lieutenant smirk that Frank grew to hate during his two years in the army. He knows Kees is daring him simply to anger him, simply to make him feel small, because he knows Frank wouldn't dare.

'You want to take a swing at me, do it. You're just a nigger to me, and there's nothing you can do or say to make me change my mind about that. So take your swing. This is your chance.'

Frank's right eye twitches with tension.

Kees's smirk turns into a smile which shows his teeth. His eyes say he knows Frank won't do it no matter how much he wants to, no matter how much he can taste it – and he can taste it, like blood, in the back of his mouth, coppery and bitter.

'I've been through too much tonight,' Frank says through gritted teeth. 'Don't tempt me.'

'That's why the Negro will never move forward. You're all cowards. You're a born slave—'

But before the cocky motherfucker who knows he'll never get hit hard by the world can get the last word out, Frank's shoulder is in his chest, knocking him back against the police cruiser's door, and Frank hears an *oof!* as the air is forced out of his lungs and hears the crunch of the window roller snapping off as Kees's back slams into it and the hollow thud of his head slamming against the water-spotted window. And then the door swings open – Kees must've accidentally pulled on the handle as he tried to push himself off the door – and the two men fall out onto the asphalt, Kees on his back, Frank on top of him, staring down at this stupid son of a bitch who thinks the world will never touch him. Frank grabs the guy by the hair and slams his head against the asphalt, and there's an ugly hollow thud, but Frank barely hears it.

'Am I a coward now, you son of a bitch?'

He slams his big fist into the man's nose.

'Am I a born slave now?'

He punches the guy in the jaw, sending his head sideways, and three teeth fly out of his mouth and skitter across the gray asphalt like loose change, another imbedding into the flesh between Frank's middle finger and his ring finger. But Frank doesn't care. He's not done yet. Even sharks die. Another punch to the cop's face and his eyebrow splits open like the skin on a sausage and blood pours into his eye socket.

'Am I?'

Another punch. And the cop is trying to push Frank

away, trying to push him off, but Frank punches again and again and again and – the cop puts a gun in his face and Frank is looking down the dark barrel and past it to the hamburgered face of the cop and murder in a pair of bloody eyes.

'I should put you down like the animal you are.'

Frank gets to his feet, backing away, breathing hard.

'Are you pointing that at me as a cop?' he says. 'You dare me to attack you, call me a coward, and then when I do what you dared me to do, what you said I was too cowardly to do, you pull a gun on me? I'm a coward, you say, but you can't even fight your own fights. You got out of one mess by letting your precinct captain buy off a man you tried to murder, and now you're pointing your service revolver at me after you said you weren't a cop for this fight. But you can't do that. Because you lose. Because without that uniform and that fucking service revolver you're nothing. Because you walk around like a fucking shark but you're not. You're a minnow who just happens to have a shark on his side. And if you pull that trigger, you'll just let your brothers in blue clean up another mess. And why not? It's their mess, isn't it? They're the ones who gave a fucking frightened minnow a set of shark teeth.'

As Frank talks – half sure he's about to get shot, half sure his brains are about to Pollock the street behind him: the cop's eyes are on fire – he and Kees walk around in a half circle, a sort of dance, repositioning physically as they reposition mentally. Frank is trying to figure out if he can get that gun away from Kees before the man decides to push a bullet into his forehead, and he can see the wheels spinning behind Kees's eyes, trying to figure out if he can get away with pulling the trigger.

But then Frank stops.

He looks past Kees to the Hobart Apartments.

He can see blood everywhere, and he sees his neighbor, Kat, lying on her side, unconscious, just outside her front door. Keys hang from her doorknob. She was driving home just as he was leaving. He waved at her as he drove past – like he was just heading off to get a bottle of milk. Has she really been there this whole time? He looks over to the courtyard and sees carnage. He swallows.

'Call an ambulance,' he says finally.

'What?' Kees says, still pointing his gun at him, still angry.

'Call a fucking ambulance.'

Then Frank, with the gun still on him, walks past Kees, right past him and his gun, and toward Kat, lying on her side just outside her front door. Blood everywhere.

Kees thumbs back the hammer.

'Don't you fucking move, you son of a—'

He swings the revolver around on Frank and Frank cringes as he walks, waiting for the bullet, but it doesn't come. He glances at Kees over his shoulder as he heads toward Kat, and he sees that the cop now sees the carnage as well, and Frank sees the fire leave the man's eyes, and he knows he's safe. For now anyway. He's not gonna shoot him in the back.

Frank walks to Kat – poor tiny, fragile, broken bird – and he kneels beside her on her front porch. She simply lies there motionless in a dress that looks like it might once have been light blue but which now is just brown with drying blood.

A knife sticks from her chest. The blade is buried all the way inside her; the only part visible, the cracked wooden handle.

Her eyes are open, but she seems to be simply staring blankly.

He reaches out to feel her pulse, but then she blinks.

'Help,' she whispers. 'Please, help . . . Frank.'

'I'm gonna call an ambulance,' he says. 'Help's on the way.'

He looks up at Kees. The man is still standing in the street, gun hanging from his arm. He is simply standing and looking at him, at him and Kat and the blood, and not with disgust or shock but with something much worse – mild interest.

'She's still alive,' Frank says. 'Call for a fucking ambulance.'

Kees nods at this, as if it's the first time he's heard the request, then holsters his weapon.

Frank looks down at poor Kat.

The knife handle throbs in her chest. It's barely visible, but it is visible.

Frank doesn't want to count – he feels sick just thinking about it – but he thinks she's been stabbed at least a dozen times.

'An ambulance is on the way,' he says.

Although it's hard to tell Frank thinks he actually sees a faint smile touch her lips.

'I'm not going to die,' she says, and it's barely a whisper. 'An ambulance is on the way. I just have to lie here and wait.'

Frank nods.

'That's right,' he says. 'Just lie there and wait. An ambulance is on the way.'

'Easy-peasy,' she says.

44

One of the things that surprised David when he first started the night shift was how often things happen at four, five, six o'clock in the morning. Before he started, he'd thought the first hours would be the busiest – from midnight till four, maybe, when many were still up and drinking – but no: everything happens between four and six. The night is alive with mischief between four and six. The world goes to sleep and evil steps out into the moonlight. Cops he's talked to have told him the same – most burglaries happen between those hours, for instance.

He is shoving his last french fry into his mouth as John pulls the ambulance away from the curb.

They've got a stabbing to attend to.

45

William pulls his station wagon into the parking lot behind the Carlson Canning Company. He puts the car in park and turns off the engine.

He still doesn't understand why no one stopped him.

He steps from the car, slamming the door behind him.

The gray clouds light up briefly, as if someone in the sky turned on a light and the filament broke – the bulb exploded – and a clap of thunder fills the air. The air feels full of electricity.

Someone should have stopped him. He knows people saw him. He saw their faces in the windows. He saw their faces looking at him. He saw their wide white eyes filled with shining interest. He saw them with their hands pressed against the glass, with their noses pressed against the glass, with their mouths hanging open.

But no one stopped him.

It makes no sense.

Maybe no one stopped him because it's what he's supposed to be doing. Maybe it's his real purpose in life. Maybe he's doing something that's supposed to be done for a reason beyond his understanding.

Multiple concussions rumble in the distance.

Don't be stupid, William, he tells himself.

You're sick, that's all. You're just sick.

He walks across the asphalt to the back stairs and walks up their concrete steps. He feels shaky with lack of sleep. He feels as if he's walking through a dream. He pulls open the heavy back door and walks inside.

He can see other employees milling about.

He grabs his timecard from its slot on the wall and stands at the back of the line leading up to the punch clock. A guy he sometimes talks to during cigarette breaks gets in line just behind him. His name is Bob.

'How's it going, William?'

William shrugs.

'You look tired.'

The line shuffles forward.

'I am,' William says, 'I am tired.'

'Long night?'

William looks back at Bob, standing there in his blue denim shirt, timecard in one hand, lunch bucket in the other. Bob, who goes home to his wife and son every day, and plays catch with his son every weekend; Bob, who probably never has urges – terrible urges in his guts like a rash inside you that won't go away unless you do what they want – and who's certainly never acted on them; Bob, who he shares cigarette breaks with. Lately they've killed the time during smoke breaks discussing the upcoming World's Fair in Flushing Meadow Park and how pathetic the Mets are.

'You don't know the half of it,' he says. Then he reaches the punch clock and punches in. He puts his card back in its slot on the wall where it belongs.

William stands in front of the conveyor belt, watching the tin cans roll by. As each one passes, he quickly scans the lid for leaks, flips it, scans the other end, and sets it back down so the conveyor belt can carry it away.

He does this silently, one can after the other.

He wonders if anyone is ever going to stop him.

46

Patrick stands in the open doorway looking at his mom.

He had hoped when he told her he'd help her she'd say no, honey, that was just talk, that was just your mother being tired and talking, but she didn't say that. She said thank you and yes. She said she was finished. Then he went to get the pills, which he'd left on the coffee table – as he had hoped he wouldn't be needing them – and he found them where he left them, sitting next to his Order to Report.

He picked up the Order to Report and read it (again); he sat down on the couch and thought about it (some more). He thought his mother was right: he'd been using her as an excuse – but soon she wouldn't be there anymore and he'd have to actually face the world.

He thinks that now, standing in the doorway, looking at mom: soon she'll be gone and he'll be alone in the world with no excuses.

He's supposed to report for his physical three hours from now, and with his momma gone, he'll have to go. It's that or jail. And while the idea of war is frightening – guns and mud and blood and grenades and shrapnel and thwacking helicopters overhead and jungle stench and gangrene and burning villages – it also seems slightly unreal, like something from a movie. Jail is very real. It's a small concrete box, and he's tired of small boxes, concrete or otherwise. The world is a big place, a frightening place, but maybe once he's seen Vietnam, maybe once he's faced his fears, it won't be quite so scary anymore. Maybe once you've had a gook shooting at you from some unseen location while you trudge through the jungle and gangrene sets in on that foot wound you got last week – maybe when you come back home from that, the streets of the city seem a little more bearable, a little less frightening. An investment banker can't possibly be as intimidating as a Viet Cong guerrilla with blood in his eyes.

Mom finally turns her head away from the window she'd been staring out of and looks at him and blinks.

'I'm ready when you are, I guess,' he says.

Mom nods.

'I'm ready too,' she says. 'How long do you think it will take after I finish the pills?'

'I don't know, momma.'

'Do you think it will hurt?'

'I don't know. I think you'll just go to sleep.'

'I wonder if I'll get nightmares before it's done. I hope not. I hope I don't get nightmares.'

'You don't have to do this, you know.'

Mom nods, but it looks to Patrick like she's nodding to herself, not to him.

'Yes, I do,' she says.

'Okay.'

Patrick walks across the room to his mother's bed and sits on the edge of it. He forces open the orange pill bottle. He dumps the pills into his hand to see how many there are. He wants to make sure there are enough.

Twenty-eight.

He doesn't know how many it will take really but twenty-eight seems like a good number. He thinks he'd have been uncomfortable with anything under fifteen or twenty. He doesn't know why. He doesn't even really know that twenty-eight will be enough; nor does he know that ten wouldn't be. But it seems like it'll be enough. It's a lot of pills.

Twenty-eight.

He cups the hand holding the pills and scoops them back into the bottle, save three. Three at a time. Gone in nine swallows save for one.

He hands the three pills to mom and she puts them into her mouth.

He picks up the glass of water. He wonders if one glass will be enough. Then he hands it to his mother. She smiles, puts it to her lips, sips, tilts her head back.

Over ten percent of the way through it already.

Patrick pours another three pills into the palm of his hand.

'Good night, Patrick,' mom says, closing her eyes.

Patrick takes the empty water glass out of her hand and sets it on the nightstand and looks down at her.

'Sweet dreams,' he says.

47

There is only darkness and the sound of sirens at first, and when she opens her eyes and lets the light in and sees the off-white ceiling pushing down on her, Diane realizes she must have fallen asleep. Fragments of dream-images still float in her head:

Picture Diane sitting on a couch. A face looking at her, white and doughy and sitting on a coffee table next to a gold watch. Just a face like a mask on a coffee table next to a gold watch. The watch hands move counterclockwise. A knock on the door and the door melts away. The face's body come to collect. The head is there too but it has no face; it's just featureless flesh. And it's come to collect.

Means nothing, Diane. Just a dream. Forget about it.

She'd like to but it makes her feel crummy. She has a sense of dread sitting heavy in her guts.

She looks at the clock – nine minutes past six.

The suitcase she packed is on the floor next to the bed. She must have kicked it off the bed in her sleep.

Dreams of running.

When she was a little girl living in a small town called Elgin, in Texas, she had a pet dog named Dinosaur. For some reason she thought it was hilarious at the time to name pets after other animals. She also had a pet cat named Horse. But it's the dog, Dinosaur, she's thinking of right now. He used to run in his sleep. He would lie on his side on the carpet in the middle of the floor when he slept and everyone would have to step over him to get from one place to another in the house and every once in a while while he slept his little feet would really start kicking and he'd bark once or twice or three times and run and run and then it would be over.

'Chasing rabbits,' dad would say.

Dreams of running.

She picks the suitcase up off the floor and sets it on the bed. Then she picks up the clothes that fell out and puts them back in and closes the suitcase.

She clicks the metal latches, locking it, puts her hand around the handle, hefts it, and walks to the bedroom door. She unlocks the bedroom door and pulls it open, hardly believing she is actually doing this.

Is she crazy?

There are worse things a person can do than what Larry did.

But, she thinks now, this isn't really about what

Larry did. Maybe if that was all she could find a way to forgive him eventually. Maybe. But there's more: there's the way watching him eat used to amuse her and charm her but now it makes her stomach sick; the way he never wants to talk about anything; the way he goes through her purse and takes her tip money so that he can go out drinking – if he asked, she'd give him some, but he doesn't even ask. Dozens of little things. That's what it's about.

She walks out of the bedroom and into the living room.

Larry is asleep on the couch, lying on his side.

He is wearing his pants and socks but that is all. His white belly, lumpy with fat, is spread out on the couch like unrolled bread dough. Gray hairs sprout in a trail from his waistline, up past his belly button, and then thin out and disappear.

The sound of sirens grows louder, but it's still faint.

She sets down the suitcase, walks over to Larry, and quietly kisses him on the cheek.

'Goodbye,' she says.

As she walks back to the suitcase and wraps her fingers around its handle she hears a sound from the kitchen. A cock crowing.

When she lived in Elgin, Texas as a little girl she used to hear the real thing every morning. They had chickens for eggs and to eat. Once when she was about seven or eight her dad took his axe into the chicken coop, a plywood structure he'd spent a couple afternoons building, and there was the familiar sound of chickens squawking, feathers flying, and then a *thunk!* as the axe thudded into the tree stump in there. Dad'd had to pull many trees out of the ground after they bought their acreage so that there'd be room to set down their little house and after building the chicken coop one of the tree stumps went in there to act as a chopping block. It was soon covered in hatchet scars and a slick layer of curdled blood.

Usually after the *thunk!* there was silence, as if the other chickens understood what they had witnessed and were mourning, but this day there was none of that. The feather flapping and the squawking continued. Then Diane heard curse words – shitfuckgoddamnitall – escape her father's mouth. A moment later a headless chicken came running out of the chicken coop proper and into the fenced-off area surrounding it. Diane had spent the next nine days stuffing grain down its headless gullet. On the tenth day, though, she found it dead. The rest of it had finally caught up with the head, which had been put in the pig's slop the day it was axed.

According to Diane's watch, it's ten minutes past six.

The clock is off, slowing down; the battery must be dying.

She thinks about writing *batteries* on the shopping list stuck to the refrigerator, just under *eggs*, which she remembers writing yesterday after cooking the last of them, making Larry an omelet before she left for work, but there's no point in that.

Instead she simply lifts the suitcase, walks to the door, grabs the doorknob, and pulls it open.

Thomas finishes the last of his now-tepid coffee in a single swallow and sets the chipped mug down on the coffee table. In his left hand he holds a brown paper lunch bag. He is afraid to walk out into that bloody courtyard but knows he's got to do it.

In the distance, but growing nearer, the sound of sirens – at a level where you almost don't realize you're hearing them, like real-world sounds incorporated into a dream that you only understand you heard once you've awakened.

'I have to get to work,' he says.

Christopher is dressed now himself, wearing his own pants, a shirt that Thomas loaned him, and his bowling shoes. He is holding a cup of coffee and sitting in Thomas's easy chair.

'Okay,' he says. He sets his coffee cup down and gets to his feet.

'Maybe,' Thomas says, scratches his cheek, continues, 'maybe we shouldn't walk out together.'

Christopher doesn't say anything for a moment. He just looks at him.

After a while he nods. 'Okay, if you think that's best.'

Thomas doesn't really know what he thinks. He's never been in a situation remotely like this before. The relationships he's had with women all felt forced and false for one thing and almost always ended as a result of apathy on his part. He just didn't care enough to – well, to do anything. And then it was over and the credits rolled.

This doesn't feel like that. This feels natural. Yet it also makes him feel guilty. But that might simply be for the reason Christopher says it is: he has been told his entire life that one should feel guilty for having such feelings and especially for acting on them. It makes his stomach feel sick. It makes his stomach feel sick but it also makes him feel happy somehow, happier than he can remember being. It makes him feel that someone else, another human being, understands the turmoil he's felt all his life; it makes him feel for the first time that another human being could possibly be a salve for his loneliness. He's been so lonely perhaps because he has spent a lifetime rejecting the only source of companionship that could have meant anything to him, the only kind of companionship that felt right.

'What if . . .' he says, and stops.

'What is it?'

'What if we walk out together? What if we didn't pretend at all anymore?'

'It will change our lives forever.'

Thomas nods.

'We'll never be able to go back,' Christopher says.

Thomas nods again. He knows that what Christopher is saying is true, but somehow it doesn't seem to matter.

'I'm tired of lying,' he says.

Christopher is silent for a long time, thinking it over, and then finally he says, 'Okay.'

'Let's go,' Thomas says.

Peter and Anne stand next to one another in the living room. They are standing a couple feet apart but they're also standing together. Peter feels melancholy despite the fact that Anne has agreed to try to work things out. He knows they will probably never get back to the place they were before last night, but maybe in time – a year, two years – they'll be able to get close.

He hopes so.

Ron and Bettie are standing by the front door. Ron's nose rests crooked on his face, bloody wads of tissue stuck in his nostrils, and Peter thinks the guy will probably have to visit the hospital. Then he remembers his broken knuckle and thinks he might have to as well.

'I'll see you at work,' Ron says, grabbing the doorknob, twisting it, pulling the door open, revealing the empty hallway which leads to the tiny self-service elevator twenty feet away, which is barely big enough for two and always smells like corn chips and socks for a reason Peter has not been able to figure out in his three years here. Three and a half years.

'I think I'll be calling in sick,' Peter says.

Ron nods.

'Then tomorrow.'

'Tomorrow,' he says.

And then Ron and Bettie step out the front door, closing it behind them. Peter can hear the muffled sound of them talking as they walk away. Usually – because the walls are thin – he'd be able to hear what they're saying, but not this morning, not right now.

Right now the overwhelming sound is the sound of sirens.

Erin Riva wakes to the sound of wailing. She sees that though it is a gray light shining in through the window morning has arrived; the sun is beginning to make its ascent. She is on the couch and her mouth tastes bad.

She wipes the sleep-boogers out of the corners of her eyes, blinks several times.

Did Frank come home last night?

The last thing she remembers is talking to him on the phone, the relief that overwhelmed her when he told her that she hadn't killed anybody, that the worst she had done was damage a child's toy, walking over to the couch, deciding to lie down while she waited. Then nothing. Beautiful sleep. She had dreams of the accident but they were only dreams – not nightmares – and waking now she doesn't have that crummy nightmare-headache she sometimes gets.

'Frank?' she says, but he does not respond.

She walks through the apartment looking for him, her feet shuffling through the place, making lonely feet sounds, and as each room is found empty, she gets more nervous.

Why wouldn't he be home yet?

He called – she looks at a clock – almost an hour and a half ago. He should be home. Even if the car broke down and he had to walk he should be home by now.

So why isn't he?

And where is he?

48

Frank looks up from Kat and sees a white Ford F-100 ambulance hooking around the corner, tilting with the momentum of the turn, straightening out, and rushing toward him and the scene, all lights and noise.

A moment later it's arrived and it screeches to a stop.

The passenger's door opens and a pale, dark-haired man in his mid- or late-thirties steps out through it. He looks like a man who's already seen too much but knows he's gonna see a lot more in his life before it's finished.

Frank gets up and steps out of the way so that the man and his partner, who is stepping from the driver's side door of the ambulance, can do their jobs.

Before the ambulance has even come to a complete stop David pushes open the ambulance's passenger door and steps out of the vehicle.

He doesn't have to ask anyone where the injured party is. He can see her before his feet hit the ground, a brownish-red blanket of blood covering her body, the same brownish-red that has been splashed all over the surrounding area – everywhere he looks he sees blood.

A colored man is kneeling over the woman, stroking her hair absently, watching him get out of the ambulance. He rushes toward him and the fallen girl and is about to ask the man to please step away when he does it on his own.

'What happened?' David says as he arrives, assessing the situation.

'She's been stabbed,' the guy says in sad understatement. The kitchen knife in her chest up to the hilt would make it obvious even if the other wounds did not. Her dress has been pushed up around her waist, and there are bloody gashes in her right calf and her left thigh. There are four bloody slits in the abdominal area. Another in the shoulder. Another at the back of her neck. Another in the small of her back. Her arms are raw, completely lacking in skin – looking like a segmented picture from an anatomy text – and David can't even begin to guess how that happened. Her panties are bloody and shoved to the side.

The colored guy must have seen him looking because he says, 'I wanted to pull the dress down but I didn't know if I'd be destroying evidence.'

David nods, moves around to her front, feels her pulse, which is weak but present.

John arrives carrying a scoop stretcher and freezes.

'Jesus,' he says. 'Is she dead?'

'Alive,' David says, and he hears the admiration in his own voice.

He does admire her; she has fight. He knows that not because she's still alive – though someone with less fight in her would have been long dead – but because of the carnage. She is a person who has refused to die, who tried to fight her way out of this situation that she was thrown into. Life in a city like this is simply one accidental run-in after another, strangers passing each other by the thousands, sometimes interacting, usually not in any significant way – howdy, hi, a stolen wallet, dropped change, excuse me, sir, you forgot your hat, eye contact on the subway, here, take my seat, I didn't realize you were pregnant or I'd have offered sooner – but sometimes when passing one another, strangers collide. Hard. It's just the way it is in a city. And sometimes it ends in death.

'Let's get her on the stretcher,' David says.

John hunches behind her, putting the scoop stretcher against her right shoulder, which is lying against the cold concrete of her front porch, and holding it in place with his legs. Then, together, David and John roll her onto her back on the stretcher – David pushing, John pulling – moving her as gently as possible.

A pained groan escapes her mouth. David is glad for it. At this point – with her in the state she's in – he's glad for any sign of life.

*

Kat can't move. She doesn't understand why she can't move but she can't. She should be able to but she can't. She can only stare straight ahead. She sees her neighbor Frank's bent knees. He is crouched in front of her and he is wearing jeans smeared with car grease. She feels his hand stroking her hair and that's good, that's nice, and she can hear him saying, 'An ambulance is on the way.' And she can hear the ambulance. It's here. She only had to lie here and wait. Then a brief conversation, and then someone is moving her, and it hurts, God, all of the wounds that had gone cold and silent start screaming again, but when she tries to scream herself it's only a barely-audible groan, and then she is on her back, and she's looking at the gray sky, the gray sky behind which, she thinks, this universe's malevolent God is hiding.

'One two three,' someone says, and she feels her body being lifted.

Things are moving. She is moving. She is being carried somewhere but she can't move her head so all she can see is the gray sky and things out of the corners of her eyes – buildings passing by and trees passing by and brief faces with shining eyes looking at her – and then she is in a small room with a white roof; no, not a room, she's not in a room: she's in a vehicle.

An ambulance – she's in an ambulance.

She's saved.

*

Diane stands in the courtyard with her suitcase in her hand. Is this what she saw when she looked out her window last night – all this brown blood? It can't be what she saw; she would have called the police.

Someone must have called them, though – police are here. But that first scream, that was hours ago.

As she stands there looking at all the blood, the lights of the ambulance flashing against her face and the complex's stone walls and the concrete and the oak trees and espaliers, she sees others walking out to the courtyard. Thomas, who pretends to be married but isn't, walks from his building's elevator. He is holding hands with another man. Christopher. She knows him. He's come over to watch baseball and drink beers with Larry. That explains it, she thinks, when she sees them holding hands; that explains why Thomas pretends to be married. Thomas looks up at her and quickly pulls his hand away from Christopher's, pulls it away almost harshly. Then she sees the kid with the sick mother. She doesn't remember his name; he's just the kid with the sick mother who sometimes watches her from across the courtyard. He walks out into the gray morning light looking dazed and his eyes are red. And the nurse. She walks out into the courtyard in her nurse's uniform and her white nurse's shoes. And a couple she doesn't know. The man looks like his nose is broken as it's planted crooked and on his face like malformed clay and a wad of bloody tissue sticks from each of his nostrils.

Diane finds herself standing out in this blood-splattered courtyard with all of them. She finds everyone looking at everyone else and at all of the blood – there is so much blood – but when any two people look at each other at the same time, when eye contact is threatened or made, something like shame passes across the faces and the eyes are dropped.

Diane does this herself. When the boy with the sick mother looks at her at the same time as she looks at him their eyes meet briefly and she feels ashamed and suddenly finds her own shoes very interesting.

Patrick looks away from the woman he saw crying in her living room last night and toward the street. An ambulance sits at the curb, lights flashing. Then two men carry some-one by on a stretcher. The girl he saw out here, the girl who was attacked. They carry her by on a stretcher and they put her in the ambulance and they get inside.

Doors slam.

Frank watches the ambulance drive away with a strange heavy sadness pressing against his chest and making it difficult for him to breathe. After a moment he turns away from the street and toward the courtyard, and there sees several of his neighbors. And Erin – his wife. Frank walks toward them, stepping over a puddle of blood as he does, and he feels the sadness and the sickness inside him turning into something else, mixing together and turning into something else completely – a strange but undeniable chemical reaction.

'Nobody saw what was happening out here?' he says, looking from one person to the next. 'Nobody called the police?'

He thinks about seeing her driving home from her job at that bar she works at, passing her, waving, seeing her smile at him; it seems like it's been ages, but it was only a little over two hours ago. He thinks of that and he thinks that she must have been out here the whole time. Her keys are still in her front door. He thinks of all this blood. It trails across the courtyard, which is lit with lamps at night. Dim lamps but lamps. Dim but bright enough to see by. Bright enough that you can see the courtyard at night even if your apartment lights are on.

Frank swallows. He is shaking. He feels his hands shaking. Too much has happened.

He puts his hands in his pockets to stop the trembling and he looks from one person to the next. Nobody looks back. They all just stand in silence, looking down at the ground.

And then the silence is broken. A man with a bent nose, with bloody wads of tissue sticking from his nostrils, says, 'We – we have to go.'

He pulls the woman he's with out toward the street, past Frank. Neither of them look at him as they leave. Neither of them look at anybody. They just walk out toward the street, the woman slipping in a smear of blood and almost falling, and then they're out of sight.

'I have to get to work, too,' Thomas says. Thomas, who Frank has always liked. How could he have let this happen and not done anything to stop it? How could any of them?

Thomas walks out of the courtyard toward Austin Street trailed by another man who Frank does not know.

'I'm going, too,' says a woman with a suitcase. And she does, she walks away.

'I picked up the phone to call the police,' says Patrick.

Frank knows him as a good kid. He takes care of his sick mother. A lot of work but he does it. Thankless work but he does it.

'I picked up the phone,' he says again.

'Honey?' a voice says, a voice he recognizes, a voice he has heard every day for the last twenty-one years.

He looks toward Erin and she looks back.

She takes a step toward him.

Frank only stares at her.

She must see something in his eyes she doesn't like because she takes a step backwards and she says, 'I'll be upstairs.'

Frank can only look at her. He looks at her until she is gone.

Even in his pockets, his hands tremble.

49

As the ambulance rushes toward the hospital, all lights and noise, David pushes himself away from the girl. Kat, the colored man called her. He pushes himself away from Kat and simply sits there in the back of the ambulance.

After a while he says, 'She's dead.'

The sirens stop wailing; the lights go out.

David has her purse, which was lying on the porch near her, and he thinks about looking through it but decides against it; seeing her personal effects will only make it sadder. Is there anything lonelier than a bent business card at the bottom of a purse with a random phone number scrawled on the back and no name to accompany it? Is there anything sadder than a single earring floating around with loose change, its partner forever lost? He didn't know her, of course, but it's always hard when you fail to save someone – even when you didn't really have a chance. And she was tough, she was a fighter, and that makes it harder.

She didn't want to go. She didn't go. She was taken.

Yeah, and that makes it harder, too.

But she's gone. She's gone, so when the ambulance pulls up to the front of the hospital, it pulls up almost silently, with just the sound of the engine and the thick rubber tires crunching over asphalt and a few loosened pebbles.

Then the vehicle stops.

David pushes the back doors of the ambulance open.

He stands in front of the hospital for a long time and looks out at the employee parking lot. He lights a cigarette and inhales, and looks out at the parking lot. He takes out his flask and unscrews the cap and takes a swallow – and looks out at the parking lot.

He is thinking again – about a pale, dark-haired boy who learned that monsters are real; about a pale, dark-haired man who learned that monsters can have gentle eyes. There is something wrong with a world where monsters are allowed to have gentle eyes.

Taking another drag off his cigarette David starts out to his car. It's a long walk. He spends most of his waking hours in a sedentary position so he parks as far from the hospital doors as possible. That way he at least gets a little walking in every day. He walks slowly toward his 1963 Chevy Nova. As he walks he sees a bolt of lightning stick its fingers into the earth and then vanish again. A moment later the thunder comes.

When he gets to his car he unlocks the passenger's side door and thumbs open the glove compartment.

He grabs the .38 caliber revolver with its two-inch barrel from its spot atop his registration information, checks to make sure it's loaded – it is, with five rounds, the slot behind the hammer kept empty – and tucks it into his waistband. He takes one last drag off his cigarette, tosses it to the ground, and grinds it out with his shoe.

David pushes into Mr. Vacanti's hospital room. There is another bed in here and a curtain to divide the room but the other bed is empty and the curtain bunched up against the wall. Morning light seeps in through the window.

Mr. Vacanti has a bloody piece of gauze taped to his forehead where a shelf of glass used to be and his left leg is up in a sling. The heart monitor attached to him beeps steadily but David is pretty sure it'll stop beeping shortly.

Mr. Vacanti turns to look at David.

'You,' he says.

David nods in agreement, closing the door behind him, walking toward Mr. Vacanti, pulling out his revolver, thumbing back the hammer – the cylinder rotating a notch – pressing the barrel against the gauze taped to the motherfucker's forehead, making the man cringe in pain.

'Me,' he says.

Mr. Vacanti stares up at him from his supine position.

'I knew this would happen,' he says. 'I didn't know it

would be you, Davey. I didn't know that. How could I? But I knew it had to happen.' He swallows. 'Before you pull that trigger, though, I want you to know one thing.'

'What?' David says, though he doesn't really give a shit what the man has to say.

'I'm sorry.'

The apology makes David feel nothing. He simply stares down at this man, this monster with gentle eyes, and wonders how many other small boys were introduced to the horrors of the world by him, how many other small boys knew too soon that the monsters of the world often aren't hiding in the shadows waiting for you to step out of the light but are standing in the bright sunshine themselves, smiling down at you and holding out an inviting hand.

'Out, out, brief candle,' Mr. Vacanti says.

David frowns.

'Only an asshole would quote *Macbeth* at a time like this,' he says.

A brief smile flits across Mr. Vacanti's face and his eyes are lit by a brief humor, and then both of those things are gone.

'You know your Shakespeare.'

'I got a book of quotations for my birthday,' David says.

And then a sound like the world cracking in two.

50

Lightning and thunder cut the sky and a heavy rain pours down through the open wound. There is no wind so it simply falls straight, crashing to the earth in little explosions.

Patrick and Frank both stand in the courtyard. They are both smoking but as soon as the rain really starts coming down Frank flicks his soggy butt away. Patrick tries a little longer, holding it between his thumb and index finger, cupping it in his hand, palm down, so the back of his hand works as a cigarette-umbrella, only taking it to his mouth for a drag.

Both Patrick and Frank silently watch cops cordoning off the area in front of Kat's apartment.

As the rain hammers down from the sky Patrick and Frank watch it wash away the blood that hasn't yet dried, which is most of it. The blood is washed away into gutters, flower beds, between cracks in the concrete, and out toward the street, leaving behind brown rings that have dried around the outsides of the puddles.

Patrick feels sick inside.

He takes a drag off his cigarette and thinks it's strange that in a week there will be no evidence that anything ever happened out here.

David walks down the quiet early-morning hallway, gun tucked away in his waistband. He feels strange, hollow. Like a husk. He reaches an elevator and takes the elevator down to the first floor. He steps out into the early morning rain. He closes his eyes and lets the rain pound down on him and wash him clean.

Lightning is almost immediately followed by the crash of thunder.

David pulls the revolver from his waistband. He empties the cylinder into his hand and looks at the bullets in his palm. None of them have been spent.

When the thunder came – with David pressing the gun against Mr. Vacanti's head and Mr. Vacanti looking up at him – the man gasped and a dark liquid spot began spreading in his sheet just below waist level and David pulled the gun away from the man's head and tucked it back into his pants and simply stared at him. He stared at this pathetic man and thought of emptying his skull of brains. Mr. Vacanti looked back with his gentle eyes. He opened his mouth to speak but David shook his head at him.

'Don't,' he said.

Then he walked away.

He resisted the urge to look back.

Now he stands in this parking lot outside the hospital. The rain falling on him is cold and makes him shiver but it feels good too.

He thinks of a small dark-haired boy pedaling his bike as fast as he can down the center of an otherwise empty street, the future ahead of him unknown and filled with possibility, steering toward a puddle and splashing through it, laughing as he rides toward whatever lies ahead.

He turns his palm sidewise and watches as brass rounds fall from his hand and clatter to the wet asphalt.

In a moment they are still.

Patrick, standing in the courtyard, tosses his cigarette butt aside and looks over at Frank.

'I'm gonna go in,' he says.

Frank nods but doesn't look at him, simply stares out into the distance. The rain is thick now, impossible to see past, and the detectives have black umbrellas out covering their heads. They stand and talk and do little else now that the area is cordoned off, but Patrick doesn't think Frank is looking at the detectives. Or at the blood that is now already mostly washed away. Or at anything else out here.

Whatever he's looking at is in a deeper place.

Patrick turns away, leaving the man to his thoughts,

leaving him standing alone in the rain, the sun now visible, its brilliant light spreading across the eastern horizon.

Patrick walks to the elevator and gets inside. He pulls the doors closed and presses a button.

The elevator jerks and begins moving.

He has to report for his physical in two and a half hours.

A moment later Frank heads inside himself. He wants to get out of the rain, at least temporarily.

But after he has changed clothes and toweled dry he finds he still has water running down his cheeks. He wipes it away with the back of his hand and walks to the bedroom where Erin is lying in bed, on her side, holding herself. They look at one another. Then, without saying anything, he climbs into bed behind her and wraps his arms around her body. He can feel her heart beating gently. She snuggles against him.

It feels good – just a little bit of human warmth in a cold world.